Eight Stories Aliens Will Believe

Stanley B. Trice

Copyright © 2024 by Stanley B. Trice
Published by Every Word Rise, LLC
Place of Publication: New Bern, NC

Cover and formatting by Woven Red Author Services, www.WovenRed.ca

Library of Congress Control Number: 2024921915

Eight Stories Aliens Will Believe/Stanley B. Trice—1st edition
ISBN ebook: 979-8-9915098-1-7
ISBN paperback: 979-8-9915098-0-0

Other Books by Stanley B. Trice

High School Rocket Science (For Extraterrestrial Use Only)

Evidence of a Commuter Train

A Chance to Tell Ten Stories

A Boy's Life with Older Sisters

Contents

THE DAILY LIVES OF ALIENS AND HUMANS 7
Finding an Alien Romance 9
Breakfast Items..19
Briefing on Cue 39
Best Alien Friends Forever....................................49

ALIEN ABSURDITY & ILLOGICAL HUMANS.......... 63
Geese Honking, Alien Imitations, and Human Cluelessness
.... 65
Human Pollution, Invasive Species, and a Planet Saved.....80

ALIEN HOPE 95
Leaning On an Alien Harvester 97
In The Beginning..105

BONUS! TIME TRAVEL (FOR SOMETHING
UNALIEN)... 123
Retirement 2039.. 125
The Disease 138

About the Author...157

The Daily Lives of Aliens and Humans

Finding an Alien Romance

Gillian was happy whenever she came home from another date without being left for dead somewhere in Atlanta. Not that the men she dated would have killed her, but she had so little in common with them that her evil side might have emerged and been enough to drive them to murder.

She walked into her one bedroom apartment that sat in the center of a cramped styled building in a crowded neighborhood within a congested suburb. The apartment was only big enough to house a three person kitchen table, a two person couch, and a single bed along with a few end tables and decorations needing dusting. At six feet tall, her living space was teaching her to be claustrophobic.

After getting ready for bed, Gillian took a glass of chardonnay and sat on her couch to watch the latest romance movie. She did not believe in romance movies, but they made her feel a little better about herself. Even though she had no romance at thirty years old.

Two years ago, she was excited to move to Atlanta for her

current job as a software engineer. She planned to have a new group of friends, more than what she had back in the miniature Vermont town she grew up in. Yet, the city was overwhelming and now she had fewer friends than in Vermont.

This included nine followers on her social pages, who were probably AI bots gathering data for future dating scams. She was content to be included in their data scouring. It meant she was wanted by someone, even if they were not real or honest or ethical.

A month ago and discouraged by her chance selection of men, Gillian had resorted to surveying dating apps. She wanted to find someone who had enough friends she could claim some as her own. Except, she found the apps matched her with men who were soul suckers or just weird and had no friends.

Being a software engineer and frustrated with her dating app selections, Gillian finished her glass of wine and decided to make her own dating app. Besides, the movie was over—happily ever after. She gave the closing credits the finger.

The next morning, Gillian got ready for work by first staring at her face in the bathroom mirror. A habit she took to clear her head of the person who she wished had more courage to declare to the world who she really was. "I wish I had a magic mirror to make me feel good at what I'm seeing," she told her brown eyes.

She let her eyes do too much exploring and spotted the wicked witch of sagging had brushed her face again in the night. "One day, I'll need a crane to keep my sagging face from making my neck disappear."

She had a sudden rush of anxiety, cautious and slight, yet there. It was the same feeling of restlessness and dissatisfaction that her life needed a change to be happier. "Did leaving my

Vermont cause all of this? Maybe I should take a trip to Oslo or Niagara Falls and get away from Atlanta," she told her mirrored self.

In the shower, Gillian chased away these thoughts as the hot water dripped off her long straight nose she got from her Egyptian father. Later, she spent fifteen minutes mangling her thick black hair into a style that made her look as if she just got out of bed and had done nothing to it. Gillian blamed her mother's Nigerian heritage for giving her too many bad hair days.

Unable to get her contacts to work, she resigned to putting on her glasses. Except they kept sliding down her nose. Each time she pushed them up, she felt as if she was punching herself in her face for not staying in bed. Gillian gave up messing with herself and rushed out the door, late.

She met the bus as it rolled away without her, making her wait twenty minutes in the warming air. The rising humidity made her sweat and a gathering crowd of commuters made her want to be alone. When she finally got to her cubicle and instead of logging onto the company network, Gillian sat there trying not to quit and run away.

She once swore her belly would never stick out any further than her heavy breasts. She looked down at herself and it was getting close. She whispered to her monitor, as if it was her only friend, "After a year, this is what cubicle living has done to me. Made me look at my body in a way that shouldn't be looked at while living in a tired gray cubicle."

"I want to be in a warm bubble bath with a glass of rich wine," she typed as her password to log on, with spaces.

Gillian spent two hours trading emails with her co-workers, some of whom sat on the other side of their shared cubicle wall. She could hear them typing a response back to her. The two hour email discussion could have been done in a ten minute conversation. But the company would not have proof of their productivity.

At ten in the morning, she logged in to a live stream video of the daily office meeting where everyone was encouraged-told to participate. On her computer screen were eight of her co-workers and their supervisor, Sam. The co-workers and she could have met in the empty conference room down the hallway, except there was no working video there to record their meeting.

Gillian looked past Sam's narrow shoulders and bald brownish head to his painting that covered one of his walls. Blue plants reached for an orange sky and green sun. Silver mountains sparkled in the distance and in the foreground was a yellow lake where gray fish popped out in play. No wonder the office gossip had Sam as an alien from outer space. But aren't we all aliens in some respect to each other? This got Gillian wondering how a real alien date would go.

Oddly, previous online searches gave little on Sam beyond the four years he was a supervisor. "Is that when you fell to Earth?" She giggled, making sure she was muted.

Gillian admired Sam's wide smile and hazel, oval shaped eyes. Also, his even toned voice. The meeting was scheduled for half an hour, yet her supervisor kept talking in a soft baritone longer than that. Gillian felt as if she was getting a massage.

Sam's voice sent Gillian wishing she could find someone like him who gave her peace with herself. A weekend ago, she thought about the video call with her parents. They orchestrated an online family reunion every two weeks with her two older brothers, their spouses, kids, and herself. The calls always gave her a tension headache.

Her brothers had more things to talk about, and Gillian felt caged inside the world of heterosexual relationships and family. Everyone was happy and living what she was told by her mother was a normal life. Everyone seemed to have criticism for her lifestyle of singledom. Secretly, Gillian was critical of her lifestyle, too.

When Sam ended the live video streaming with a happy hand wave, she whipped out her smartphone. It took multiple flips through her apps to find the dating app she used the most. She wanted it to be hard to find and discourage its use. Except it was too easy to find since she knew where it was and had used it too much lately.

Gillian studied the app's design and layout. "I can do better," she told the app. The audio was off so the AI couldn't talk back.

Each night that week, she used her software experience to design and build a dating app that took her in a different direction from what was popular. Sam's office painting inspired her to explore all possible paths. She wanted a relationship with someone who did not have to be a man or human. She wanted someone different who would take her beyond a current life.

"I need my database to include those not from Earth. Maybe I'll have a better chance with an extraterrestrial," she said to her glass of chardonnay that Saturday night.

An alien romance intrigued her. She thought it could be something to keep her at odds with her family's restrictive views. She hoped there would be yelling to get everything out in the open.

That night, she video called her best friend Nora in Vermont. They had been friends since middle school when Nora believed aliens had abducted her when she was five and seven years old. Gillian believed Nora who said aliens were every-where living as regular people in society. She liked Nora as a friend because she could be right.

Nora kept Gillian connected with Vermont. She lived where she always lived, and Gillian could never decide whether that was good or bad. It was just Nora, she con-cluded.

"Have you been drinking or taking drugs? So, you made a dating app to date an extraterrestrial like those triangular headed grays in flying saucers?" Nora looked up from slicing carrots on her kitchen island. Gillian could see and hear in the background her friend's six and eight year old sons and hus-band at the kitchen table talking about schoolwork.

"Maybe I might be exaggerating things a little. But I'm thirty and haven't met anyone I'm compatible with or even who I like enough to touch." Gillian looked out her second floor apartment window. The only window she had. It showed sunlight strength fluorescent lights keeping watch on children playing in the playground. The nearby parents looked young, which made Gillian frantic. She was getting too old to look at young parents with children.

"So, you think the only logical conclusion is to find some-one not from Earth? Could it be that you need to meet differ-ent people other than who you are looking for here on this planet?" Nora finished the carrots and stared into the video. "You were always more excited with women you met."

"Have you had snow already in Vermont?" Gillian missed the white stuff. It was the cold that gave her pain. Along with Nora's truths.

"Not yet. It hasn't been cold enough. If you come back, I bet you can find a teaching job. Maybe in the same middle school where you and I first met as students."

The thought of going back made Gillian desperate to finish her dating app and stay where she was. "There's enough people from my past who never left. That's way too many people I would have to apologize to if I came back. But if my app doesn't work, I'll let you know."

Late that night, Gillian watched a romance movie with a sub-subplot of alien contact. The movie made her want an alien romance that included a happily ever after. She finished her dating app on Sunday and went to work the next day to test it since the network was faster. At quitting time, Sam walked past and smiled at her.

Her supervisor smelled so good, and Gillian wanted to kiss Sam just then. Yet, she swore not to date someone from work, especially her boss.

An hour later, Gillian finished testing. Actually, she was tired of messing with the app and uploaded it to the company's network. Several weeks ago, she discovered the company had a satellite dish capable of bouncing a signal off the International Space Station and into space. Gillian had no idea why they would need this, but she was glad to find it.

She sent her dating app into outer space confident someone out there would be interested in meeting her. Gillian was excited when a few minutes later the signal struck the International Space Station. From there, it would travel to Jupiter's moon Europa, and eventually Saturn's moon Titan. She read how Europa and Titan had the best chance to host life in this solar system.

She went home and video called Nora. "I did it. I made my dating app."

"Great. Is it live?"

"Yeah, but it only goes into outer space."

"Explanation, please."

Gillian hesitated. Nora was taking off her makeup in the bathroom. "I made it to attract only extraterrestrials."

"I thought you were joking."

"No. For some reason, my company had a link through the ISS and into space. I feel good about this," said Gillian.

"You know I believe aliens are on Earth already. Maybe you should try to find one here."

"If they are here, why didn't they answer any of the popular dating apps?"

"Would you know if they did? Anyway, you need to come home to Vermont. It's not too cold anymore. Maybe you can find an alien around here. Vermont has so many unnormal and unusual people," Nora said, with half her makeup off or still on.

"Maybe you're right and the cold isn't that bad. If I come back, can I stay with you for a while? It's horrifying to think of moving back in with my parents. My brothers would be all over me about it."

"Yeah, of course. We have an extra guest bedroom with a separate bathroom. You won't have to share it with our kids."

The boys worried Gillian. She wondered how she would adapt to a family that was not hers. It might make me panic to find someone too soon and have my own family before I'm ready, she thought. There was a deep hesitation in her mind.

Later and before she went to bed, Gillian checked her dating app. A messaged blinked anxiously for her to open it.

"Hi, I'm an extraterrestrial. At least temporarily. I'm Carolyn on the International Space Station. You want to meet for some coffee and a scone when I fall back to Earth in a month? I know a cozy café in Boston. I'll send the dates and location. If you're straight and only like men, I'm cool with it. We can still be friends. But I guessed from your app that you're like me. A loving person looking for someone different and alike at the same time."

Gillian remembered reading about Carolyn when she first arrived at the station months ago. She declared to the world, "I was always afraid to admit that I liked my own sex until I saw our borderless, blue planet. I am no longer afraid."

When the ISS passed over and communication was better, Gillian emailed, "I want to know everything you've seen that gave you the courage to be a loving person. I'll be there for that scone."

Then Gillian sat on her bed and had a good cry. She felt much better and texted Nora about Carolyn. Nora called thirty seconds later.

"Tell me everything."

After they talked, Gillian said, "I need to come back to Vermont. I don't have anyone to talk to here, and I'm always sweating from the humidity."

"What about your family?"

"I'm going to tell them I will love who I want to love. They can keep their beliefs and I'll keep mine."

Gillian hardly slept. She felt an overwhelming relief and strength to face her family, live her life like she wanted, and enjoy whatever relationship she would have with Carolyn.

In six days, Gillian quit her job, sacrificed her deposit to terminate her apartment lease, and sold everything she could not carry in five suitcases. With the compact car over packed, she sat in her empty apartment to check on her dating app again. There was another response. She closed her laptop instead of reading it. "I feel good about meeting Carolyn." Her voice echoed in the empty room.

The first morning when Gillian was no longer at her job, Sam sat at her cubicle before anyone came to work. Sam knew all about Gillian's alien dating app and was disappointed when she accepted an invitation from a temporary alien without looking at the second response.

In the cubicle, Sam used alien senses to breathe in Gillian's leftover body odor. She had a fragrant, spicy aroma that reminded Sam of home. "Why didn't you read the second response which was mine? You would have loved my planet. We have a beautiful green sun that gives us gorgeous orange skies with shiny lavender sunrises and sunsets. Also, on my planet I am female. We just look like the males on your planet."

Sam heard one of the staff coming to work and she tipped toed to her office. She closed the door and sat in the swivel chair where she spun herself around over and over making herself dizzy. It was a feeling of fun from her childhood that helped her relax. She felt as if she was flying through the universe.

After a few minutes, Sam stopped spinning and used her computer to connect with her planet using the International Space Station link she created as a booster. It helped her reach the dark energy around Jupiter. From there, the signal zipped to a nearby star system hidden from Earthians by dark matter.

"I'll simply link Gillian's dating app with my dating app. I am positive there are more humans who will be excited to have an intergalactic relationship."

Sam went back to spinning herself in the swivel chair. "Now that I met Gillian, I am sure there are more people like her on Earth who will love me for who I am, and I can love them for who they are. Even if we are from different planets."

Breakfast Items

When astronomers and astrophysicists detected dark energy, which was expanding the universe, this led aerospace engineers to replicate the energy on a miniscule level. Soon, rocket engines could propel spaceships at almost the speed of light. This became less important when the same technology could find and peer through the curtain of dark matter, which was holding the universe together.

Three light years away, astrobiologists discovered a thin layer of dark matter hiding a solar system with a Sun-like star and nine planets. One planet swung around the star at a similar distance to Earth.

As humanity was prone to do, they visited the planet and found it so much like Earth that the inhabitants were so much like humans. Except they looked as if they could be breakfast food.

Anthropologist Denise was on the eleventh spaceship to visit the planet Buffet, which the inhabitants called it. Data from previous missions gave her enough material to communicate with the inhabitants during her four month visit of study.

The family she chose met each crisis without yelling or drama. When she left on the spaceship, her mother and older brothers expanded on their resentment toward Denise for not staying. Their religious beliefs held that leaving Earth meant she was not a child of God anymore. Her dad celebrated his daughter's adventure off the planet of too many wrong opinions about beliefs and God.

Now back on her spaceship orbiting the planet and with the crew preparing to leave in five days, Denise had only to complete her report. She tied her coarse brunette hair back in a ponytail to control the curls, turned off the AI input, and used her humanness to write the true story of the family she fell in love with.

One evening, Pancake's wife Syrup of four years got up from the sofa to answer a knock on their apartment door. They had a rule, at least he did. When eating together, one of them would not eat without the other. Pancake gave Syrup his most annoyed look, but she was not looking since she had left to answer the door.

He sat on the sofa staring at his TV dinner cooling on his TV tray while his favorite sitcom bathed the compact living room in flickering canned laughter. From the doorway, Pancake heard Syrup not hesitate to let a young woman's voice step into their one-bedroom apartment. Pancake was suspicious. At this hour of night, if this woman stayed they only had one bed.

He heard the young woman say, "This is a critical period in my life and I need my mommy."

It took a few moments for Pancake to lift his round, doughy body and face the two women at the front door. Pancake stared at his wife. "You have a child?"

"This is my quarter century old daughter Egg," Syrup said, holding her daughter's hand.

"You told me about your husband dying in the black rock mines. You never mentioned having a daughter. Where has she been until now?" Pancake could not look at Egg just yet.

"Egg knows this, but I was pregnant when I got married. It was what everyone did back then. I met Egg's father at my high school graduation and right after the green aliens who raised me for the past six years left to return to their planet. They were good to me and I understood they had to leave. But I was lonely," Syrup used her teary eyes at Pancake.

"Please, not the teary eyes. When your husband died, why didn't you find your family?"

"My only family was my dad and he was still messed up from my mom dying from cancer, which is why he gave me up for adoption. After my adoptive parents, the green aliens, left I felt lost. Then, some blue aliens came and wanted to raise Egg," Syrup said, smiling at her daughter. "I knew they would be as kind to her as the green aliens were to me."

Pancake held his palm up to stop Syrup from any more explanations. "This is too much for me. I haven't finished my dinner."

"I'm sorry, but I've been holding all this back for so long and I should have told you about my daughter and now you know and I'm sorry you found out this way."

"Hi, I'm Egg." She held her hand for Pancake to shake, which he did clumsily.

Syrup wrapped her skinny arm across her daughter's shoulders. "I was scared for my Egg and happy those gentle blue aliens took care of her. I wanted the best for her and I've always kept in touch."

"My mom came to all my school events and softball games. It was great. And now I need her even more since my adoptive aliens had to leave for their home planet, just like my mom's."

The two women flung their skimpy arms around each other and Pancake did not understand how they could ignore him singing a chorus of disbelief. They broke their skinny embrace, still ignoring him, and sat on the living room sofa. Egg sat in Pancake's spot.

He stared at the young woman Egg who had a broad face, brown eyes, bulbous nose, and thick lips all scrunched in the middle of her face like a yolk. Not unattractive, but attractively unique.

Syrup's long, thin face looked like a drawn out drip of thick goo ready to fall on something flat, round, and doughy like him. At the moment, she was dripping sweet words of empathy on Egg and paying no attention to him. He stood there not knowing what to do with two upset women in the living room. Syrup had turned the TV off.

The two women created a high-pitched chatter that sounded like butter sizzling in a hot pan. This irritated Pancake, since he was not a sizzler and they continued excluding him. He took his TV dinner and went to the kitchen counter where he watched the sitcom on a compact TV. Syrup liked the show more than he did and he turned it off when he finished eating.

Pancake was not sure what he felt worse about. Having a stepdaughter or that his wife kept this important piece of family news a secret from him. Pancake told Syrup about his son Bacon in the first twenty minutes of their first date.

His two decade and three year old son was living for the

past five months in the small town playing his alto sax in front of the most popular, and only, coffee shop hoping to be discovered. Although the town had barely enough people to be discovered on a map.

Pancake was happy Bacon moved down from the black rock mountains to the valley where he and Syrup lived. Syrup was happy, too. Now here was Egg. Would they all continue to be happy?

With mom and daughter continuing to chatter toward each other, Pancake took a peanut butter and mustard sandwich to bed. He drowned the sandwich down his throat with a glass of ice water and felt better when finished. He hadn't made a mess on himself or the bed.

Pancake sat up trying to read his poetry book while ignoring the women's splay of words through the apartment. He was not successful. Fortunately, the chatter lasted only twenty minutes.

Syrup smiled coming into the bedroom. Before darting into the bathroom, she held her fingers in a V as a peace sign, then touched her lips for her husband to wait for her. Fifteen minutes later, she came out of the bathroom and climbed into bed.

"You know I don't like to talk about serious subjects in bed, but I have to say something or I'll have trouble sleeping," Pancake said. "What other secrets are you keeping from me? You knew all about Bacon who's living nearby."

"Egg is asleep on the couch, so we have to whisper. I'm sorry for not telling you about her. I wanted to, but I couldn't and I didn't and I should have. I'll tell you in the morning why she needs me. Right now, I need you." Syrup leaned over in bed and gave her husband a hefty hug and a wet kiss.

He wished he could be angry, but he knew this was his wife

Syrup's way of explaining things and he loved her for it.

In the morning, Pancake came into the kitchen as Egg came back from getting her own coffee from the coffee shop. She placed a tray of bagels, donuts, and pastries on the kitchen table before leaving again without saying where she was going. Pancake struggled to make a selection without coffee, which was still perking.

When the coffee finished and before he could pour a cup, Syrup jumped into the kitchen and slammed her open palms down on the table. The food leaped from the excitement.

"She's losing herself," Syrup said in a monotone voice she would use when upset.

Pancake disliked the monotone. Especially without coffee.

"She's got breast cancer and is getting a radical mastectomy. How am I going to save her from having only one breast?"

Not wanting to continue upsetting her husband, Syrup stood by the table and sang in her soprano voice about her worries and anxieties over Egg. After about eleven minutes and with Pancake's stomach hungry and no coffee to clear his thoughts, Syrup blew out a final sigh and sat down.

Pancake poured them a cup of coffee before sitting down and saying, "Sometimes people lose things and they're still okay."

Syrup took a deep breath, grabbed a plain donut, and shredded it on the table. She ate half of the crumbs. "She'll walk around lopsided with only one breast."

Pancake was not sure how having one breast could change a woman's walk. He thought about how he would probably walk the same if he lost fat in one of his fatty breasts. "Aren't you having lunch with her today?"

"Yeah, I have to know about what's going to happen so I

can worry about her properly when she loses her breast. I need to take care of my daughter. She'll be lopsided and can go topless only on one side. How is that going to look? I'm sorry, I'm talking all mixed up."

"Egg seems to be healthy and strong, despite having cancer," said Pancake. He did not understand the female body. His body was large enough he could lose a lot and not realize it. With a sip of his coffee, he picked a blueberry bagel. Blueberries were healthy.

"She's always been healthy, not counting the cancer. Will she be healthy afterward? I can't be healthy if she isn't," said Syrup. "You need to get to work. Don't forget the lunch you made last night. It looks good."

They both knew Syrup was good at breakfast, but not lunch or dinner. Pancake stood and shifted his weight into his thrift store jacket as Syrup straightened out his sloppy appearance. She smiled and slipped her long-fingered hand across his wide cheeks. Her touch was like maple syrup falling slowly across the face of a buttermilk flapjack.

Her long, thin face went lost in Pancake's round cheeks as she kissed him goodbye. "Remember, bigness is your signature," she said.

Denise took a break from writing to release her thick curls. They danced on her shoulders as she looked out the spaceship's window. They circled in a low orbit and below her the blue green seas and brown red foliage drifted past her window like a clock ticking.

By the time she got back to Earth, almost half a century would have passed due to the time dilation of traveling close to light speed. Her mother already sent a message that her dad had died a year after she left.

Denise figured her mother would likely be alive when she got back to Earth. Her brothers had married and had two children apiece and would be there, too. She had wanted her dad to welcome her home. He was the only one to see her off. They understood each other. Denise never understood her mother or brothers and they never understood her.

She considered not going back. Also, she would be a great aunt to someone and she was too young to be considered old and great.

Pancake drove his three decade old, faded blue pickup two blocks to the Crystal Clean Movie Theater he managed. He also owned it, which he pretended not to. If the city condemned the theater, he planned to call his dented pick up a new form of junk art. That way he could sell it for a lot of money and pretend he was retired, at least until he needed to go back to work.

When not playing his sax, Bacon worked the snack counter and kept the theater clean. Pancake could only afford movies in the public domain, so the movie watchers were well into their retirement careers and forgettable messy.

Running the projector gave Pancake something to do besides watching the theater deteriorate and worrying about where Bacon would live if the city condemned the building. At the moment Bacon lived in the loft that smelled less than the basement where Pancake used to live before meeting Syrup four years ago.

At two in the afternoon, Pancake walked out of the movie theater as the second matinee began. It was a horror, romance, drama, mystery type of movie that made people laugh and cry. He considered the risk of relying on AI to keep everything running. Bacon had left to play his alto sax some place where he could find people who liked saxophone music.

Pancake kept reconsidering his actions as he drove one block to the city's library, a renovated elementary school. Inside, he met walls of dust covered books poised to be read by a local population who did not read books much.

Syrup told him a year ago that the library held secrets. Pancake struck across a wide reception area of flaky carpet and sunk his bulk into a flimsy wire chair hoping to find those secrets.

In front of him was a small, dingy antique monitor at least five years old. He stared at finger smudges from people thinking it was a touch screen. Fingering the keyboard, Pancake quickly found himself linked to data sources from places he did not know existed.

He searched for Egg. "How long had she been in town?"

Pancake asked the monitor these questions, but it was not audio controlled. He typed the words across the monitor and had two typos that were not autocorrected. Fortunately, he knew how to correct the words without AI help.

He stared into the smudged glass of a computer monitor, not even a flat screen. He wanted the blinking images to explain how Egg posted messages on the theater network for Bacon. "I work there and I don't know how to do that."

Pancake became distracted and went over what happened more than six years ago after the divorce from his first wife.

Bacon was seventeen and the courts forced him to live with his mother and new husband on top of the mountain. It wasn't long before Bacon found refuge staying with Pancake in a small cabin at the foot of the mountains. Pancake would have stayed there with his son except he needed money to stay there which meant, after two years, he had to leave.

"Can't you come with me?" Pancake asked Bacon the morning he was leaving.

"I need my mom to love me."

"Your mother left me for that man. She said she never loved me, nor did she like me." Pancake did not tell his son any more. He wanted him to have hope.

In a database, Pancake found a history of the theater. After leaving the mountains, it was the first place he found a job to stop his leaving. The town was in a semi-mountainous piedmont region and if he had gone any further there would be the ocean. Deep, turbulent water scared him.

Pancake found forty year old photographs of the theater when it was new and fresh. With his income, there was no hope for that look again.

For the first few months, he lived and worked at the theater, rarely going anywhere so he could save money for an apartment. At the end of those few months, the owner died. He detested his family and left everything to Pancake. The owner's family were good with that since they considered the theater a liability. Pancake went out to celebrate at a breakfast diner, which was where he met Syrup who was his waitress.

Another database listed their marriage four months later in a courthouse setting. They agreed it was needed as soon as possible so they could get on with loving each other more. That same day, they moved into the apartment they still live in.

Pancake dialed into another database where he found the event bringing Bacon to live in the theater. When he moved out of the cabin four years ago, his ex gave the bank's loan officer a supply of street drugs, something Pancake refused to do. The loan was written off and the deed transferred to Bacon's mother. Pancake knew it was a ploy to keep Bacon near her and away from him.

"I know that, dad," Bacon told him after the transaction. "I know you love me. I need her to love me, too."

Four years later, Pancake read the police report about how a mountain wind blew his ex's single wide trailer, along with her husband, three hundred feet down the mountain. When the funeral happened, Bacon came to live in the theater with Syrup's overly encouraging encouragement.

Now there was Egg who would keep Syrup here with needs, wants, and unknown beliefs about living with one breast.

Even with shifting his butt in the creaky library chair, Pancake's size hung out on all sides. There were few seats he got comfortable with. Staring at the monitor, he returned to his search for Egg through multiple databases. Yet, when he clicked on the next file the monitor blanked out. All his work disappeared into a black universe.

Pancake stared at the curved glass and squinted his eyes, but that did not help bring back the images. He looked up and, halfway across the reception area, he spied a stooped, gray-haired man sitting behind a faded tan counter. This man's facial features, doughy with age, looked flaky as if from a history of time and heat. To Pancake, the man belonged in a library with old books.

The letters for 'Reference' spit across the front of the counter with the missing 'f' and second 'r' making it look as if someone was screaming or swearing or praying. The reference librarian staggered into a standing position and approached Pancake while dragging his wire chair behind him.

The scraping legs put grooves in the already groove filled carpet, as if the librarian did this several times a day for the past hundred years. The librarian pushed the metal chair up beside Pancake, or as close as he could. Pancake's wide girth consumed all available nearness.

"Name's Biscuit," he said, raising his fatty arms and slapping his pudgy fingers across the keyboard.

Words and numbers reappeared and peppered the smudgy monitor in a logical, readable order that made no sense to Pancake.

"You're calling up stuff about you. I was researching stuff about my stepdaughter Egg, who my wife Syrup gave up for adoption. Egg showed up yesterday with breast cancer and I didn't even know Syrup had a daughter."

"Be patient. It'll lead to something," Biscuit said.

Pancake eased back in his swivel chair that threatened to break as Biscuit tapped on the keyboard. He was a fast typer. Maybe forty words a minute fast.

Biscuit had an average size that would be just average, with no particulars of any concern. The older man could blend into a crowd of tall men and short males and join the average high point on a bell curve. Pancake thought how he was big enough to be unnoticed only if there were brontosauruses there.

As Biscuit's arthritic looking fingers prowled across the coffee stained keyboard, Pancake puzzled over how coffee stains got into a library that did not allow beverages. He watched Biscuit's pecking fingers pull up a handwritten account of Syrup as a teenager. How long had that information been in a forgotten grave of archived electrons?

"It says here that aliens abducted your wife Syrup when she was three, five, and seven. They were a different breed from those that visit us now. They were the gray triangular heads who thought people were happy being abducted," said

Biscuit, pointing out the words in Syrup's high school year-book.

"Those are her favorite numbers and she always liked triangles," said Pancake. He could not read the handwriting, so it had to be Syrup's.

Biscuit stared at the information, taking deep breaths. He kept his hands on the keyboard, preventing Pancake from taking over.

"Who are you? How can a dirty monitor show this? Is my wife an alien from outer space? She said she was adopted by aliens at twelve years old."

Biscuit took his hands off the keyboard. "You want to hear about Bacon? I can tell you now or in my next life if we meet again."

"How do you know about Bacon?"

"This is a library."

"Was he abducted, too? No, I don't want to know. I know too much about him already," said Pancake.

"There's more information about Syrup," said Biscuit.

"I want to know about Egg. Let me finish my research." Pancake waited for Biscuit to leave, now that the computer was working.

Biscuit's bones cracked as he pushed away from the monitor. "I think you should lay flat and not be consumed by what Egg or Bacon do. They'll sort themselves out in the end." Biscuit stood up and grabbed the back of his chair to drag it back.

"What else can I do?"

"Make it last,"

"Make what last?"

"The taste of you with Syrup. You're big. You're lardy. Let Syrup lather you. Let her melt into and want you over and over in sweet layers. You've got a lot to cover and it'll take everything she's got. But, give her some time to be with her Egg, who is good with Bacon." A tear scampered down Biscuit's rumpled cheek as his slumped shoulders barely held him up.

"How do you know all this? What's wrong?" Pancake asked.

"I'm her grandpa." Biscuit stared at Pancake.

"Whose grandpa?"

"Egg's. Syrup is my daughter who I gave up for adoption when she was twelve years old. Our wife and mother died from a quick cancer and we were messed up being together. I worried that with another abduction, my daughter would volunteer not to come back. Those green aliens said they would protect her. But I never abandoned her. I secretly went to her school events, her prom, high school graduation, wedding day, was in the hallway when Egg was born, and at the funeral of her husband."

"Why didn't you help your daughter with Egg afterward?"

"I didn't want to add to her emotional troubles. So I contacted some blue aliens who wanted to help. It took me too long to get over my wife's death and I think I'm getting there. Maybe soon I'll meet Syrup and Egg. Just not now," Biscuit said.

Pancake did not look at the monitor. He rolled out of the swivel chair and stood up, trying to keep from falling onto the floor. "How many breakfast relatives do I have? What is it with your family giving each other away all the time?"

Biscuit said nothing as he dragged his wire chair back to his Re_e_ence station. Pancake looked out a nearby window.

"It's dark outside. How did I sit all day staring at some piece of glass and forget the time?" The movie he left running would have run out hours ago and the retired people, with no place to go, could still be waiting for the next movie.

Pancake's mind was torn between going to the theater or home. Syrup might want to know what he did all day, he needed to know where his stepdaughter Egg could be found, and was Bacon still playing his alto sax somewhere? These decisions were immediate problems that made him hungry.

Halfway to his desk, Biscuit looked over his slumped shoulders and said, "Fill your stomach early in the morning with a good hearty meal and you'll last all day. And a little more advice."

"You've over advised me already."

"Make yourself become something simple and good. Like the mix of a little flour, some cream, and maybe a pinch of salt, but in a blender for a wild ride."

Pancake dashed out the door. Except, his puffy size made it look as if he was walking fast. In his worn pickup, he drove past several closed breakfast restaurants until arriving at his apartment. He figured his theater patrons would have left since the snack bar was closed. Stepping in the apartment, Pancake smelled pesto sauce burning and watched Syrup stirring boiling pasta next to the burning pot.

"You were always better at making breakfast," Pancake said, stirring the sauce in hopes of saving it. The spiciness erupted across his face.

"I'm not good at doing two things at once," Syrup said. "You know what's the secret of life?"

"I didn't know there was a secret. I thought life was just was."

"The secret is to keep from becoming a zero. Live life as if you were at least a number one," said Syrup.

"This is leading to something."

"I didn't tell you, but months ago I found that Egg had

followed Bacon down from the mountains. They have been living together in the theater."

"How did Egg and Bacon meet?"

"After high school and community college, she worked at a music store, which was where she met Bacon."

"Bacon told me he met someone and I kept waiting for him to tell me who." Pancake wondered if he should have asked.

"I kept going to the movie theater to talk with my Egg and I should have told you, but I was afraid she would run away and become a missing person statistic."

"We're all statistics in some database." Pancake wondered how many databases he lived in.

"I paid for her to go to the doctor when she felt the lump. I think Bacon and his sax will do Egg some good and make them taste like they belong. They like it in the theater attic," Syrup said to the pot of boiling pasta. Steam rose into her face like a white veil.

"I'm sorry I married Bacon's mother. She liked dinner too much. The only thing we had in common was a tequila worm while sitting in a theater on a Saturday afternoon. Except, I'm glad we had Bacon and I always admired him for trying to save his mother."

"I left the black rock mountains to get away from another relationship with a miner. None of them liked sweets, anyway. I'm glad I moved because I found you," said Syrup.

"We need to stop keeping secrets. I didn't tell you, but my parents gave me up for adoption when I was ten to some orange aliens. My parents wanted to travel and they let themselves be abducted by the gray triangular head aliens. I was angry they left me behind. Yet, I will always love the orange aliens who took care of me. They accepted me for who I was and loved me for that."

"You never told me about them."

"Like many of these aliens, my orange parents had to leave. They left after I graduated from community college and I was okay with that. I know they are out there in the universe thinking about me," said Pancake.

"On the night of my high school graduation, my adoptive parents told me how much they loved me, but they had to leave. Our planet Buffet was killing them. I was scared to be alone. I married Egg's father out of resentment, then I had Egg at nineteen. I shouldn't have been so rash and rebellious. Egg's father was a drunk and a zero and I was still a teenager. Now Egg is my hero. And you, too. Also Bacon, who loves my Egg." Syrup stopped stirring the pasta and let the steam bathe her face with warm moisture.

"You heard of a man called Biscuit?" Pancake turned off the sauce and threw some ice cubes in to give the burned flavor some hope of being less burned.

"He's my dad who gave me up for adoption." Syrup dumped the pasta in a drainer and left it there draining in the sink as she sat at the kitchen table. "I know he works at the library. He doesn't know I know."

"He might know now." Pancake sat at the kitchen table across from his wife.

"I promise I'll stop keeping secrets from you. When my dad left me with my adoptive parents, I knew he did not run away. I saw him at all my school events, my graduation and wedding, he followed me home after Egg was born, and he stood among the headstones at my husband's funeral."

"Why didn't you go up to him?"

"My mom's death scared him with grief. I know he loved me in his own way and just knowing he was around was enough for me. I think one day he'll come out of hiding," Syrup said.

Pancake reached across the table and held his wife's hand. "Maybe you could check the reference desk for a good book."

When Denises' spaceship left orbit to return to Earth, she returned to the planet Buffet. She set up her living pod near the small town and the next day bought the theater. She also paid too much for Pancake's pickup that he called a new form of junk art, although it was just an old pickup. Denise wanted Pancake to be happy. She missed her dad, who was a lot like Pancake.

There was no hiding that she was an alien and no one seemed to care. "Brown splotchy aliens have the coolest color," Egg told Denise.

She became a member of the small town's social. She wrote in her journal about how Egg lost both breasts. "I'm glad not to wear a bra for one breast," she told Denise after the hospital stay. "And look. My hair is growing back heavy and curly and blue green. I like that better than the white and yellow."

"At least you aren't lopsided," said Syrup, holding her daughter's hand.

"Yeah, and I will always like Bacon's sax playing with or without breasts," she told Bacon who stood nearby fidgeting.

Two months after buying the theater, Egg had recovered enough to help Denise and Bacon renovate the theater. The first renovation was the theater attic for Bacon and Egg. Pancake and Syrup were happy to help.

The rest of the renovation did not take long with other breakfast families helping to create a smaller theater surrounded by craft shops and a pizza parlor. Pancake worked at the parlor and made the pizzas taste like breakfast. They were a hit. One morning, he asked Denise about her home planet.

"Breakfast is the most popular meal in the universe. At least my dad thought so," said Denise.

"Why did you leave your dad and come to our planet?"

"It had always been my dream to go into space. When my turn came, I was torn whether to go or not. I knew my dad would not be alive when I got back. He convinced me to go and escape my mother and brothers and their weird religious beliefs. He wanted me to escape humanity's opinions that were based on no facts or data. Mostly he wanted me to go on the adventure he wished he had gone on."

Outside, a bright orange sky layered everything in the color for the upcoming day. Denise enjoyed how the sky's color changed throughout the day. It helped her stay excited to wake up on the alien planet Buffet.

"I'm glad you're here. We've had aliens visit our planet and you're the only one I've known to stay. I'm glad you did. How's the pickup driving?"

"It's going to be the center art piece after the renovations are finished." Denise smiled. She did not say that her journal about Pancake and Syrup would be hidden in the pickup's glove compartment for future generations to find.

From selling the theater and pickup, Pancake and Syrup gave Bacon money to start his music career. He bought a ticket to the most famous musical auditorium within a day's drive. He snuck on stage before the main performance and played his sax for three minutes and twenty-two seconds until security escorted him off. That was long enough for a record producer to pay him to perform on her private yacht.

Bacon got seasick and threw up on the producer. Egg was there to trade dresses with the producer. Egg was all right wearing Bacon's vomit. They were pregnant and she figured it was good practice for when the baby came. The producer booked Bacon for eight months, so he would be home for the birth of his daughter.

A month before Pancake and Syrup became grandparents, Denise watched Biscuit and Syrup eat an anchovy and fried egg pizza at the parlor. It was eight in the morning before anything opened and Pancake wanted Syrup and Biscuit to talk and be a family. He and Denise stood in the kitchen listening.

"After my parents died in the black rock fields, aliens adopted me. That's why I thought it would be all right for you to be adopted." Biscuit took a bite of eggy fishy pizza.

"You don't need to explain. We're good. Besides, Egg has been into genealogy and she found out about the aliens visiting our planet. They all left journals about their lives in the library for future research. It includes information about the planets they came from." Syrup ate around the anchovies. She motioned with her forefinger for Pancake to join them.

He liked anchovies better than she did. Pancake waved at Denise to join them. "You're part of our family, too."

Denise gave Pancake a hug.

"Breakfast is the happiest time of the day," said Pancake.

Briefing on Cue

The owners of the private conglomerate company The Aliens Are Not Coming had specific goals. They wanted to offer more services, which produced nothing, by ending product lines which did. To accomplish this, they had an apparent endless amount of cash to buy profitable product line companies where they became unprofitable departments of the company. However, lately some of their directors had reversed this trend and made the product lines profitable.

This is a story about one director who did not do this. He was successful in making all the departments he directed become unprofitable, whether they provided services or products. He demanded his staff call him the Director.

When he came to work that morning, the Director strutted past his staff and found a white envelope taped to his office door. Inside the envelope was a single paper with a typed note from the Resource Committee requesting a budget briefing in two hours.

They were part of the elite executive committee who ran the company and all its conglomerates. This committee controlled all the money. The Director felt dizzy from excitement and nervousness that he may control much more than any of the other directors who he hated.

Every Wednesday, the directors were required to meet for lunch in the company's private dining room in the musky basement. The Director attended, first because it was mandatory, and second, so he could listen to their gossip. Reading the note, he realized that one popular gossip was that the company executives would give someone significant control over the company's money. He felt this was his chance at fame.

The Director spun around and faced the cubicle farm. He yelled at his staff to save his life. Shaking the paper in the air, he called a meeting in the conference room.

Looking at the sullen and bored faces, the Director quickly read the note and demanded, "I need to be successful in this budget briefing. If this is important to me, it is important to you. My success is your success."

The Director stared at his staff, who stared back.

"What are we supposed to put in this budget briefing?" This was from his lead staffer.

Her presence made him feel vulnerable. She was younger, like the other nine people he supervised. He detested all of them, yet mostly his lead staffer.

Her dark curls and brownish skin reminded him of his only girlfriend when they went to the university years ago. They shared a lot. At graduation, she dumped him for his best friend. He resented women like his lead staffer ever since.

"That's what you're being paid for. Just make sure it is no more than three pages and has no numbers in it. You know I hate numbers." The Director was careful not to call his staff names. He disliked the human resource officer, whose visits were annoying.

"Why did they leave a note on your door and not send you a priority email or call you into their office?" Another question from his lead staffer. If he replaced anyone, she would be the first.

Without answering, the Director stomped out of the conference room to stand in his office doorway with his hands on hips like Superman, his favorite superhero. He felt he was on the brink of being the company's hero if he could get his staff to save him. After making sure they were working on the budget briefing, or he hoped they were, he stepped into his office and closed the door to wait.

He had no windows, just four tan walls and a white ceiling to contrast against a brown tiled floor. He stood facing his maroon door with his feet slightly apart and his arms folded across his chest. Focusing on his breathing, his meditative stance helped him not jerk open the door and scream at his staff to hurry up.

After fifteen minutes and before his patience ran out, the lead staffer tapped on the door once before pushing inside. She thrust at him three pieces of paper.

The Director looked at his red speckled hands holding the white papers. He feared that if he failed with the Resource Committee, these people he supervised could take over. Particularly this lead staffer. "I will succeed," he whispered to himself.

"What did you say?" She crossed her arms tight across her chest.

"I understand me."

"I don't understand you. If you have any comments, you

know where to find me." She blew out a sigh, spun around, and stomped back to her cubicle.

The Director slammed the door closed with his shoe and breathed easier with her gone. At his executive desk that consumed half his office, he spread the pages across the clean surface. He admired the lack of numbers, which always frustrated him. And the few words created plenty of empty white space on the papers. The Director knew this would keep the Committee members from asking questions. He despised people questioning him. They made him feel as if he was failing.

Leaning back in his leather office chair, he told his briefing papers, "When I succeed, I will control more money than anyone in the company. I'll be more important."

From his middle drawer, the Director pulled out a single paper with the bios of the Resource Committee members he would brief. Strangely, there was little information, as if their pasts were a secret. Their bios read more like a mission statement for the company.

"I don't care. I can be smarter than them without knowing who they are."

The Director rubbed the edges of his desk repeatedly until his palms felt warm. The anticipation of briefing the Committee made him want to pee. From behind his trash can, he pulled out a wide mouth, half gallon mason jar, unscrewed the lid, and sent a dash of yellow urine into the glass vessel.

When finished, he swirled the liquid around, fascinated by what used to be inside his body. He believed the sloshing urine was telling him that success was certain. "After this briefing, the people in this company will remember me forever. I'll have a legacy." He noted the jar would need emptying soon.

Putting it back behind his trash can, the Director spun around and used a gold chain to pull down his computer monitor from the ceiling. He commanded the screen to display the photographs of the three men who made up the Resource Committee.

Their white shirts and black ties exaggerated their narrow bodies and bulb shaped, bald heads. They had a greenish hue to their skin, which the Director thought came from bad lighting. It was their coal black eyes that concerned him the most. He worried about those eyes staring at him during the budget briefing.

In a challenge, the Director leaned his long thin face an inch from the screen and said to the photographs, "I will romance each of you into believing that I am the best director this company ever had. No, no, no. None of you will remember my three years of service and product lines that lost money and failed. Those projects were destined to fail when I took them over, despite their previous success. I can prove it if I get more money."

The Director wanted to be the company's hero. He leaned back in his chair with his hands clasped behind his head, fantasizing about the status he would be granted.

Last night when he left his office, he was unaware he would give such an important briefing. He went home to his sparsely furnished, one bedroom apartment in a building too old to be converted to condos.

As he finished his supper of buttered rye toast and sardines, the Director worried about being forgotten in the company. As he did most evenings to ward off this fear, he repeated into the empty tin can, "I am important."

He repeated these words as if they were a prayer to himself

as he took a bottle of merlot to the toilet where he sat and let his bowels relax. Sitting there gave him peace with himself. He did not have to hold back on anything and he let everything go while gulping the bitter sweet, red wine.

With half the bottle gone, the Director made a bath of water so hot his skin hurt. He finished the wine as the water cooled, then slipped into bed naked under cotton sheets where he slept through his nightmares about failing. His parents became the center of his nightmares.

The Director woke up thinking he did not have enough alcohol. Three years ago when he visited his parents to announce his promotion to director, his father criticized him for not having a better job title. His mother complained that he was a disappointment for not making more money.

"Just look at the horrible life I've had with your father. He never made enough to satisfy my wants," she told her son.

"Having a woman around like your mother can make you less of a man," his father warned his son.

The Director wondered if having a sibling would have made things different. He would never know since his parents explained how he was a mistake and, like the old cliché, they did not make the same mistake twice. The Director swung out of bed.

Except the nightmare kept haunting him as he got ready for work. Finished, he thought about his loveless parents as he stared into his full-length bedroom mirror to make sure he looked good. He resented sharing the same features as his Peruvian mother, who called him five months ago.

His Irish father was driving them to their mountain ski chalet and she wanted her son to listen to their argument and decide who was right. The Director had long ago stopped caring about their arguments or about them. Before he could end the call and stop listening to his parents' pointless bickering, he heard his father yell in anger, "Shut up. I'm tired of arguing with you." His mother screamed they were driving off a cliff.

The Director listened to ugly curses, ripping metal, shattered glass, and mangled cries of pain until the phone went dead. He went to work that day, feeling good about himself. When the police called to confirm they were dead, he did not tell them about the phone call.

Twenty minutes before the briefing, the Director allowed three of his staff to enter his office.

They lavished adoration on him with yeses and praise for his three budget slides that had no numbers and plenty of white space. They told him how his budget briefing would be an outstanding success. The Director loved this false love from his falsely devoted staff.

When it was time for his budget briefing, he stomped through the cubicle farm he reigned over, saying nothing. The Director continued down a narrow hallway with confidence that this was his destiny. Success is mine, he told himself.

He had never been inside the executive conference room and was startled at the auburn colored, paneled walls and light blue ceiling. The floor was marble and the click-clack of his heels against the rock surface distracted him. He tried not to slip and fall.

The three six-foot tall, skeletally thin resource men stood behind a long brown lacquered table with a copy of his budget briefing before them on the table. Their hairless, pale heads shone in the overhead lights and their thick, dark eyebrows looked as if they were painted on. He realized someone had altered their photographs to make them look almost normal. In real life, they weren't.

There was no other furniture in the room—no chairs or podium for him to place his briefing slides on. They did not invite him to approach the table. The Director stood five or seven steps away, took his three page budget briefing out of his folder, and fumbled with the papers while trying not to slouch. He held his folder with his notes written on the inside cover as he dropped the briefing on the floor.

The Director picked up the three loose papers with no page numbers and could not remember what was the correct order. The staring, black eyes made him eager to start. He wished they would look at the briefing instead of him.

He read from one of the briefing papers, forgetting what he was going to say with this one. His folder with his notes had fallen on the floor. He rambled on about the programs he oversaw as the three men stared at him without expression. The Director wanted to scream.

With the next slide, he realized he was repeating himself. He went to the third slide trying to think of something different to say when the middle man raised his hand to stop.

"We have no questions." He had a squeaky voice.

The Director nodded his head too many times, glad they did not ask him anything. They were such strange, odd looking men. He felt a little scared.

The three men said nothing for thirty seconds. Instead, they stared at the Director, who disliked being stared at with those black eyes. They looked as if they were talking to each other without talking. After thirty seconds and before the Director said something he would regret, the men of the Resource Committee smiled and gave him a thumbs up.

Their thumbs bent backward, pointing at themselves. Their smiles were frightening enough that Wes Craven would have been scared. All the Director saw was the bent thumbs he hoped meant he was successful.

A short pale, fleshy man drifted into the conference room from a side doorway. He had too much black hair on his head, like a thick wig. He announced, "The Resource Committee is pleased with your progress. You will have more resources to achieve your project goals."

The Director could not think of anything to say. Finally, he blurted out, "All of you are intelligent, heroic leaders."

The three men nodded once, at the same time. The Director could not take any more smiling and nodding and staring. He clenched his papers, picked up his folder, and darted out of the conference room, eager to be away from all that weirdness.

He dashed through the cubicle farm, ignoring his staff's questions about the briefing result. He would make the announcement in a few hours as he handed out layoff notices. With more money, the Director could outsource their work and not have to deal with their nonsense wants and needs, and that human resource person.

After the sweaty, nervous Director left, the three men of the Resource Committee clicked double tongues into their alien language.

"This company has so much money and influence that when it fails many economies will fail, too," the fleshy staffer proclaimed.

The three men and fleshy staff person laughed. To someone from Earth, it would sound like a Jamie Lee Curtis scream.

The alien on the right said, "That human now has more money so he can continue to succeed in his failures and overcome our successful directors. His flawed ego has given him a special talent to make even our service providing departments unprofitable. Plus, he will contract with outside sources and make them unprofitable, too. As soon as we put additional humans like him in positions of controlling more money, the economic failures will increase."

The left alien said, "With so many failures, confidence in this species fragile economy will fail. It will be easy to control these humans and dominate their odd society. This will give us the opportunity to take over and discard their nuclear weapons, give them cleaner energy sources, and stop them from destroying their planet with pollution."

"It's amazing no one caught on to our company's title. The aliens are not coming, we are here," the fleshy staffer chuckled, which sounded like the gagging reflex.

The middle alien said, "With a cleaner and safer planet, more aliens will visit and be a great tourist spot for travelers coming through this part of the galaxy's arm. I envy the humans. Being service providers, they will make a lot of money if they can be nice to aliens."

Best Alien Friends Forever

Pauline's parents overdosed when she was five years old. They never yelled at her or each other when on their highs, which they called "taking a trip." Pauline figured they finally found a trip worth staying on forever. She was mad they did not take her.

A big breasted woman leaned over Pauline to explain their deaths. They faced each other in a windowless, beige room with an unused simple table and plastic chairs nearby. Pauline was afraid the curly black haired woman would topple over and suffocate her under those blobs of flesh.

Her few aunts and uncles were already in jail or unable to care for themselves, so Pauline went on trips through foster homes. This made her madder that her parents left her behind with strangers and no one appreciated her blend of screaming. She demanded to be in a permanent family.

Her misadventure happened where abandoned tobacco funded mansions sagged under the weight of rodent home life. Nearby, the Atlantic waters no longer held fishable incomes. All of this made the local populace have a money limited life and the only ones who could pass the adoption test claimed they were aliens.

The adoption services thought this meant somewhere away from the flat marshy land where they all lived. In a way, this was true. At six years old and a few weeks before first grade, Pauline agreed to be adopted by people who claimed to be from the planet Joy.

After she unpacked, they explained how their planet had crystal blue oceans, light periwinkle skies, and at night their green and red trees sang cheerful songs so everyone could sleep peacefully. Pauline hoped to visit one day so she could have a decent night's sleep.

To Pauline, her adoptive parents looked normal with their purple skin. They came to the breakfast table and drank a thick white syrup to change their skin color to a soft brownish shade or a gentle pale complexion or something with a rich ebony sheen. It all depended on the skin color of the people they would meet later that day. They said people were happier talking to people with the same skin color.

Pauline never understood why skin color mattered that much. Her parents did not understand, either. They just wanted people to be happy.

Pauline wished she could change her olive skin to something that matched her outfit. Maybe to a burgundy or emerald green, colors she enjoyed wearing. Her parents were not sure what her skin color would be if she drank the syrup. Also, she did not want her long reddish, twisty hair—a look she liked—to change. Anyway, the syrup looked yucky.

Pauline was happy with her unadventurous, quiet parents. In the morning, they stared at their separate monitors for more video talking than typing. Sometimes they met humans in the blue dining room of their house. There was a lot of talk about giving kids more permanent homes through adoption. Pauline thought her parents were heroes for trying.

The best part of her parents was late afternoon when all three chased dragonflies across the wiry grasses in their front yard. Pauline did not fear the mosquitoes floating around. Her parents attracted them and giggled at the tiny bites.

Afterward, they sat on the porch drinking sweet tea and Pauline would ask them about adopting another kid. They said they were new to Earth and would consider it. She hoped whoever they adopted was as different as she thought she was.

In her first two years of elementary school, Pauline learned how special her alien adoptive parents were. She listened to the gossip about a girl a few years ago who claimed to be raised by aliens. There was too much ridicule and laughter for Pauline to ever admit the same.

The girl and her adoptive parents relocated to the state's largest city to be lost in the population. Pauline did not want to be lost. That was how she felt with her biological parents when they took their trips.

By her third year of elementary school, Pauline collected a few casual girl friends to hang out with between classes, at lunch time, and during after school events. But not for sleepovers. She had to protect her parents and she would be expected to have a sleepover, too. It all worked out since she was a hero to some girls for not having brothers.

When she turned nine years old in fourth grade, Pauline did not like how her girl friends grew overly developed emotions. They clashed with her own erratically developed feelings and she worried about exposing her parents by mistake. She considered trying out boys as friends, but they acted more alien than her parents.

Pauline became the shy girl and stayed off the honor roll by getting an average grade in at least one class. That kept her unnoticed and helped distance her from the casual friends she pretended to have. She felt safe with her parents.

At ten years old, Pauline started fifth grade. This being her last year of elementary school, she worried about going to middle school next year. It would be an environment she struggled to imagine and she feared her parent's identity would be exposed by her saying something stupid. This was much more likely with her approaching puberty.

Over the summer, her mom tried to understand her changes by helping Pauline try on training bras. She kept them in her bureau. Pauline wanted to prolong the changes to her body as long as possible.

Riding the school bus that first morning of fifth grade were a few middle school girls. Their school was nearby. Pauline listened to them talk about their period with hate and love. Mostly hate. They were all thankful for having a best friend to go through it all with. Pauline knew what she had to do.

At supper that evening, she explained puberty to her alien parents who had turned back to purple for bedtime.

"Our people do not have this puberty experience. Do the boys have it, too?" Her dad's face looked as if he was going to throw up from Pauline's description.

"No, and it's not fair."

"It seems like the worst part of this is the period mess," said her mom. "So, how can we help?"

"I heard the older girls on my bus say that having a best friend helped. That's what I need. I need to have a best friend."

"What exactly is a best friend?" Her dad looked better.

Pauline used her fork to twirl her tomato sauced pasta in circles. "I never had one. I read online that they're someone I can laugh and cry with and we understand each other almost perfectly. We will share secrets and be honest with each other. We could talk for hours without getting bored."

Pauline's mom smiled. "I have computed what are best friends. This is something many species have. What is your proposal?"

Pauline popped her head up from her twirling. "Great. I think it's time for everyone to know who you are."

"We are good with telling everyone. We kept it a secret for you," said her mom.

"I don't need to keep it a secret anymore. I want both of you to come to the Saturday school dance as your alien selves. Whoever does not run away will be my best friend."

"We are not doing that. Humans think aliens are here to take over. We are here to enjoy the pollution humanity is making. Our planet's air is too clean," said Pauline's mom.

"Yes, if the humans want to avoid an alien invasion, all they need to do is clean up their planet," her dad said.

"Do not worry. I have an idea that will help you find a best friend," her mom said.

Pauline happily slurped a few noodles, splattering tomato sauce on her napkin tucked in her collar. Her parents did the same on their napkins. They all laughed.

That Saturday as they were ready to leave for the dance, Pauline kept asking her mom how she and her dad were finding her a best friend. Standing at the front door, Pauline's parents pointed at the spare bedroom doorway. Emerging with a broad toothy smile was a boy Pauline's age. He had sandy flat hair and crystal blue eyes.

"This is Jordan. He can help you find a best friend," Pauline's parents said in unison.

"Whoa. Who is he? And why is he coming out of the spare bedroom?" Pauline stared at a boy as thin as she and as tall, which wasn't very tall or too thin.

"We keep the transfer portal in the bedroom closet," said Pauline's dad.

"I'm ready to find you a best friend. This will be fun!" Jordan's two wiry antennae wiggled out the top of his head.

"What are those antennas?" Pauline wondered about Jordan's pale skin. She didn't want kids think she was friends with a vampire.

"They help me hear your strange language. I can hide them, but I hear less. Although, that may be good since you humans talk a lot." Jordan retracted his antennas into his flat hair.

"Is he from your planet?" Pauline eyed her dad for the answer.

"Yes. He is our biological synthetic robot we just had constructed," said Pauline's dad with a proud grin. "He has a copy of all our thoughts and memories, so he is up to date with everything."

"You could consider him your brother," her mom said with a loving smile.

"Instead of your parents revealing their alien state, I will reveal mine." Jordan smiled, satisfied he knew what to do.

"I don't know about this," Pauline looked at Jordan, and he did not look like a robot.

"Give Jordan a chance. I think everything will work out fine," said Pauline's mom.

Pauline looked at everyone before saying, "Fine. I don't

know what else to do."

In the car ride to the dance, Pauline wished she had worn her red dress and not the light blue jumpsuit that made her look older. Jordan had on a green pullover with a collar and blue jeans that made him look younger. She did not want the kids to think she was babysitting him.

Stepping into the gym decorated for the fall dance, Pauline disliked the fast new zip zap music the DJ played. "We're not dancing to that," she told Jordan.

"What happened to disco music?"

Pauline rolled her eyes and said, "Those are my casual friends over there. I'm going to introduce you as my visiting cousin. Calling you my brother would involve too many questions and suspicion. Okay?"

"What's a cousin?"

Pauline sighed. "Let me talk first. Then follow my lead."

She walked over to where her friends were sitting. There were no seats and none of them stood up as Pauline introduced Jordan, who had followed her.

"Have you been sick or something?" Tatum gave Jordan a rapid inspection with her brown eyes. Her long black wiry hair was in three ponytails with the points dyed yellow.

"He's been away and didn't get much sun," Pauline said. Yellow was her least favorite color.

"Been away where? To the dark side of the moon? And is he a cousin on your dad or mom's side?" Toby was Tatum's friend who Pauline disliked. He was shorter than most kids and used that as an excuse to be a bully. Pauline thought he was just obnoxious.

"He's a cousin and that's all." Pauline panicked. She wished she had a better story prepared to explain Jordan.

"Where is he visiting from?" Ajax had splotches of coarse black hair growing in patches on his face. Another friend of Tatum who told everyone he was turning into a werewolf.

"Why aren't any of you dancing?" Pauline changed the subject and pointed at the dance floor. Most of the kids were girls discovering their hips with the boys standing along the wall liking their discovery of hips. She spotted the parents taking turns avoiding the erratic music by stepping outside.

"You're funny looking," said Ajax, pointing his finger at Jordan's thin face.

"Yeah, you look like an alien from another planet," said Tatum.

"Does he talk?" Toby grinned and elbowed Ajax as if it was a joke.

"He can't hear you with all this awful music," Pauline said loudly to be heard over the irritating sounds.

"I like this music. I'm going to tell the DJ to turn it up," said Tatum with a sneer.

"Yeah, that way Jordan has no chance of hearing us talk about him," Toby said, grinning.

Pauline tightened her lips in anger at the three maybe not friends. She spied Jordan eyeing the three kids with wide eyes and his tongue sticking out as if he was going to lick them.

"Hey, look at that. The Jordan creature has a tongue," Ajax said with a giggle.

"Is he trying to smile? He's looking even funnier," said Toby.

Pauline faced Jordan. "They're making fun of you. Are you hearing any of this?"

"Is what they say upsetting you?"

"Yeah, and they're making me mad. I think we should go."

"I did not hear them. Wait a second."

Before Pauline could stop him, Jordan extended his antennas until they were swinging in the air over his head. There was no doubt they were really coming out of his head.

Pauline watched the three jump from their seats with wide eyes and open mouths. All three knocked over the folding chairs as they ran out the exit, yelling it was an alien invasion. No one heard them over the music.

"I can hear the music better. I can dance to this," Jordan said.

He took Pauline's hand and dragged her to the middle of the dance floor. Those not dancing spied Jordan's very real antennas and fled the gym yelling about an alien invasion. Only a few dancers stayed.

"I recognize that DJ. He is Clarence who played this music while I was waiting to arrive on Earth," Jordan said.

"So, he's an alien, too?" Pauline struggled to keep pace with Jordan's footwork.

"No, he is a robot. I learned he travels all over this part of the galaxy playing different kinds of music. I think it was your parents who invited him."

Pauline did not think she would ever get used to the music. She was already breathing hard. "How long are you staying?"

"Your parents said you needed a friend to help with your puberty. When is it over?"

Pauline stopped dancing and dragged Jordan by his shirt sleeve away from the DJ. "What? My parents told you that? You were to help me find a best friend. Listen to me. Puberty is what women go through and it's a big personal thing. I'm not sharing any of it with you. And to answer your question, it won't end until I'm old."

"Great, I would like to grow old with you. You are a smart person and I am adjustable."

"I need to find a best friend who is female and human. You can't understand what I'm going through being who you are. No offense." Pauline was not about to share her puberty with Jordan.

"No offense taken. I'll have to download a lot of data to understand the developing female human like yourself. Even then I don't think it'll be enough."

As if on cue, the robotic DJ Clarence played something soft and slow, sending five of the sweaty dancers to migrate around the drink table. The rest scattered throughout the gym in clumps of gossip to gossip about the other clumps of gossipers.

Pauline envied the five thirsty girls who splashed each other with sprinkles of sugary drinks. Adult supervision had gathered outside to calm the kids yelling about an alien invasion.

Standing alone in the middle of the gym listening to the slow tempo music, Jordan said, "What about one of those five humans playing with their drinks as your best friend?"

"Two of those girls ride my bus to middle school where I'll be next year. I don't know about the other three girls. They look like they're in high school." Pauline wondered why they came to the dance. She got suspicious with Jordan so easily pointing them out.

Jordan smiled at Pauline. "Let's meet them. Then we can all be friends."

"I don't know about this. I've never had friends like them and I don't think I'll fit in. Besides, they're having too much fun by themselves." Pauline grinned at them flicking their drinks in the air and dancing under the sprinkles coming down. They weren't worried about ending up with sticky hair.

Jordan strutted toward the five with his antennas swinging over his head. Pauline stumbled after him thinking she should go home and forget about having a best friend. One girl with blue eyes and frizzy black hair brushing her shoulders stopped splashing. She greeted Jordan and Pauline with an over-the-head wave. Her broad smile stretched across her freckled face. "Hi, I'm Gemma."

The other four peppered their names at Pauline and went to taking selfies of their sticky hair. This left Pauline wondering what to say with Gemma's cheerful smile.

"I'm Jordan. This is Pauline. She is getting ready for puberty and needs a best friend."

"Shut up. Why would you say something like that? I'm sorry for him. He's new to everything," Pauline fumbled with her words.

"It's all good," Gemma said, pointing at Jordan. "I like your antennas."

"They're not decoration. They're a part of him," said Pauline, waiting for Gemma and her friends to run away.

Gemma grinned. "Yeah, I figured. I used to live here and go to this school until I told everyone my adoptive parents were aliens."

"Wait, so you're the one with the alien parents that people made fun of?"

"Yeah. Now, I'm back as a ninth grader at the high school with two of my friends here. My other two friends are eighth graders in the middle school across the parking lot."

"Why are you back?"

"My parents are taking over the adoption services in the tri-county," Gemma said, stepping away from the four and their shrieks of laughter.

"Do your friends know your parents are aliens?"

"They're cool with it."

"Are they adopted by aliens, too?"

"No, they live with their biological parents and siblings."

"Weren't you worried about coming back after what happened?"

Gemma stepped closer to Pauline and Jordan to make it more of a private conversation. "I was scared when we left. People were angry that we were different. I don't think they ever thought my parents were extraterrestrials, but aliens from another country. After moving away, I got to thinking about those angry people and I think they were scared about not being smart enough to understand us. I'm glad my parents came back and that I'm here again."

"Those people who chased you away are still around."

"I don't care. I'm now old enough to realize how shallow and shellfish they are. They aren't even responsible enough to take care of their children, which is the reason my parents came back."

"My parents are aliens, too."

"I know. Our parents are from the same planet. No one wants to change the people who live here. Everyone wants it to be safe for us and others who live here," said Gemma.

"I've been stressed about people finding out about my parents. I feel better with you here," Pauline said, teary eyed.

"Don't get frustrated if people still don't believe you about your parents. Besides, is it really that important what they think?"

"What about your friends? You said they know about your parents and probably mine, too." Pauline watched them make faces at each other for their smartphones cameras.

"Their parents are working to bring more aliens to Earth as adoptive parents. There's a need in this area with the drugs and poverty and too many narrow opinions from the humans living here."

"Why would aliens want to help humans?" Pauline wondered how many aliens were involved.

"Just like humans, people on other planets have a desire to help and they love to be around children. It makes them feel good. They come to Earth because there is more of a need than on their planet."

"Why did you come to this dance with all of this?"

"To meet you. I don't want you to go through with what I went through alone. Besides the puberty thing, I know you have a lot of anxiety over middle school. I know because I've been there."

Pauline looked around the gym filled with chatter and nervous shuffling of kids doing a social dance with their small clutch of friends. Everyone appeared to struggle to be different from who they were. The DJ with his yellow bowtie stood in front of his display of electronic instruments as if recharging himself.

"Did you know this?" Pauline turned toward Jordan.

"Yes." Jordan said with a broad, proud smile. "This is amazing. Gemma can be your best friend and I can be your puberty friend."

Gemma giggled and Pauline stared at Jordan wondering what to say. Jordan continued with his big smile, "I can adjust myself and grow old with both of you. I discovered there is a new adventure after puberty called menopause. That will be fun, too."

DJ Clarence spun a fast song across the gym floor. This time it was disco flavored. Gemma took Pauline's hand and led her to the dance floor, followed by the other four girls. Jordan joined, dancing solo between the couples.

Pauline felt free dancing to the music. She felt as if a heavy blanket had been lifted from her. She danced with Gemma, then Jordan, one of Gemma's friends, and back to Gemma. It all felt good.

Alien Absurdity &
Illogical Humans

Geese Honking, Alien Imitations, and Human Cluelessness

George used sudsy soap and a wide sponge to scrub bird poop off the blue and yellow metal sign of the Fun Fun Water Park. He wondered why the geese liked to poop on this sign in front of the administrative building. They could have pooped on the red brick building, which was plain and could have used some colorful geese poop.

Going for another dip of sudsy water, George looked down and saw a bunch of aliens no taller than his hips looking up at him. He wondered if they came to help him clean the geese poop off the sign.

Several of them explained that they were space aliens as they reached up and placed a bright yellow stone into his sweaty palm. As the little aliens scurried away, he held the stone in his left hand where the tiny round angles felt smooth and the yellow color looked expensive.

The bright yellow stone seemed to help George think better. He felt his frantic thoughts settle down enough so he could start to sort them out. Except, the more he turned the stone over, the more it confused him. George wondered if he was holding the stone or if it was holding him.

Bored with the confusion in his mind, he slipped the stone into his top coverall pocket, which was when he forgot about it and the aliens who gave it to him. He went back to cleaning poop off the sign with his sudsy sponge when a flock of geese flew overhead. They littered the metal sign with more poop. George got some on his right shoe.

"I wish we had made George shorter," complained an alien with two left feet and two right hands. Very natural for her species.

"Or made him look less doughy, round, and cuddly. Also, his thick long yellow hair hides his neck, which I thing is George's best feature," said an alien with no neck.

"At least the yellow fuel will be safe with our simulation George until it's mature enough to use. Those noisy geese won't suspect him of having it and steal the fuel from us," said another alien who had two right feet and two left hands. Also, very natural for his species.

"Poor Bernard. He was a decent pilot until he got confused by the honking geese. It's too bad he used all our fuel to land in those pine trees across the parking lot." With all the hair, the alien looked like a werewolf.

"Bernard should have done the translation upgrade. Then we would have known the geese were confusing us to steal our spaceship fuel," said a manly alien with the prettiest face.

"I checked our database and the geese spaceship cannot be

repaired." This feminine looking alien had the most handsome face.

"At least we were able to convert Bernard into that yellow dust so he could grow into more fuel. That's what he gets for signing a contract saying we could do that to him," said an alien who looked like a thin balloon.

"We should've given our simulation model George more broken thoughts in case he learns to repair himself and find out who he really is. It will be hard to disassemble him after the fuel is matured. He might think it's murder." This alien had big teeth, thick lips, and a wide smile that looked happy, in a terrifying way.

The troupe of aliens headed to a far corner of the parking lot where their spaceship sat hidden among scrubby pine trees. They had barely passed the first row of parked vehicles when an alien looking like a balloon ready to pop stepped in front of the troupe and pointed toward the administrative building of the Fun Fun Water Park.

The aliens turned around and spied the human Jane walking from the far end of the parking lot, past George, and toward the administrative building. They could not miss her head of black curls praising her long nose and square chocolate face. The aliens chattered among themselves, wanting to know what Jane would do if she found out she gave birth to their fuel, who used to be Bernard.

At four that morning after having the best poop she ever had, Jane felt anxious to go back to bed. Laying there with the bathroom light on, she was troubled for forgetting to flush. Getting out of bed, she spotted several eerie looking, three foot high creatures pulling something out of her toilet.

She would have screamed, except she thought she was

having a nightmare. As she sat on the bed, the strange beings scurried out of her apartment door, making sure they locked it. That was when Jane realized she had been awake the whole time.

She went into the bathroom to find yellow dust around the edge of the toilet bowl. The dust looked the same as the yellow spicy flavoring that appeared on her sardines she ate before going to bed. The sardines tasted funny, but she was hungry. She remembered putting more ketchup on the little fishes to hide the funny yellow flavor. At the toilet, Jane used toilet tissue to wipe away the yellow dust and flush it down the toilet.

She was suddenly exhausted and went to bed. In the morning, she packed herself in a light blue pantsuit and rushed to work at the Fun Fun Water Park. She had trouble forgetting her nightmare.

Jane parked away from the pine trees that looked unstable and headed up the long sidewalk to the water park's administrative building where she worked on accounts payable. She dreaded going to work. Her workload was increasing as the park developed more debt to be payable.

She stepped past a fleshy guy wiping geese poop off the metal sign. Looking back, Jane spied the little beings from her nightmare coming across the parking lot toward her. She would have screamed, except they looked too funny.

"What are you?" Jane held her hands up. They stopped between her and the strange pudgy guy cleaning the sign.

"We're aliens and our spaceship crash landed. We were in your living space this morning getting our yellow fuel out of that bowl of water where you deposited it," said an alien who looked like Daffy Duck.

More of the aliens showed up and Jane motioned with her

palms for them to step back. Like her dad, she always believed in aliens and wanted to meet one, but maybe not like this. She was deciding what to do next when the reflection of the brightest yellow she had ever seen caught her eyes.

About fifty steps away, the pudgy guy at the park's sign held a yellow stone toward the Sun like he was studying it. Jane watched the odd looking aliens swing their tiny fists at a patch of large geese flying overhead.

She ignored everyone as the guy held the yellow stone higher. She felt a flood of motherly emotions flush through her with an urgency that the yellow stone was hers. Jane ran as fast as she could for the yellow. All she could think about was how that yellow thing was what she pooped out that morning. It belonged to her as if she had given birth to it.

"Stop, let me explain," said a one eyed purple alien.

"No, that yellow rock is mine." Jane kept running.

The alien easily kept pace with Jane. "We saw you yesterday after our spaceship crashed. Your body radiated a rich blend of chemicals that matched what we needed to fertilize our Bernard. We changed him into that yellow dust you ate. Your body made Bernard into that yellow rock. George is protecting it from the geese until it matures into our fuel. Everything will be all right very soon."

George remembered the yellow stone in his pocket when he felt it call his name. He pulled it out and held the stone toward the sun like it wanted. George forgot about washing the poop off the large metal sign.

"I'm Bernard," sang the yellow stone.

"Hi Bernard," George said to the yellow stone in his sweaty hand.

"I'm becoming rocket fuel. Only you can hear me."

"That's neat. You're my secret friend," said George.

An alien with antennas sticking out of their head ran up to George. "You'll have to give Bernard back to us when he's fully developed, which should be soon."

"I like yellow. Maybe I want to keep Bernard," George said to the alien.

"George, listen to me," said the yellow stone. "I was a pilot and now I'm the yellow stone you're holding. Bring me to my spaceship. I'll tell you what to do when we get there."

Memories erupted inside George's head and he knew the spaceship was among the pine trees on the other side of the parking lot. He turned around to see a curly haired woman approach. He thought the curls looked soft.

"I'm Jane and that yellow stone is mine." She pushed away the annoying little aliens with her feet to reach George. She only cared about getting the yellow stone before those strange little alien people did or the geese flying overhead.

An alien with three noses that together looked like a mouth shouted, "You can't take our Bernard away. Yeah, you gave birth to it, but we need it as fuel for our spaceship."

George held the stone over his head as everyone watched it grow slightly bigger, a little yellower, and develop sharp angles. Jane missed grabbing it from him as two aliens climbed up her pantsuit to stop her. She gave her hips a few swings and they flew off. Overhead, she spied the geese making a swoop toward them with fierce honking.

"Everyone stop fighting. What do those geese want?" Jane waved her arms at the geese to scare them away.

"They want to go home like us. Their spaceship crashed and they built another one, which they hid in the basement of the administrative building. They need our fuel, except there's only enough for us," said an alien who looked like they could be a movie star.

The aliens shouted and waved their fists at the geese, who circled to swoop down on them. George looked at a miniature, beautiful alien who looked like Gina Lollobrigida with dark eyes and brown curly hair. George knew the actress because of the old movie channel he picked up while cleaning the metal sign.

"How did I pick up an old movie channel? Hey, wait a minute. Am I a simulation? Hey, I'm a simulation!"

"George, you're a simulation. The geese will turn you off once they get the fuel from you. Then they'll create a crisis with their poopiness and scare the humans away from this building so they can launch their spacecraft," said Gina.

"I don't want to be switched off and forgotten about like in some short story," said George.

As the aliens were busy yelling and jumping around to scare away the geese overhead, Jane grabbed George's hand and tried to pry the yellow stone out. Being a simulation, George sent a light electrical shock into Jane's hand and she jumped back rubbing her palms. Not knowing what else to do, George ran toward the pine trees and the spaceship. As he ran, he felt like he was fading away.

Gina yelled to George, "Wait, George. Something's wrong. My sensor shows the fuel is sapping away your energy the wrong way."

"What's happening to me?" George kept running while looking behind him to see Jane catching up.

"Keep running. I'm getting stronger. When I'm at full strength, I won't let you fade away," Bernard confided to

George.

George heard a chorus of honking overhead. The sky turned into a rain of white poop that dripped down across the parking lot. George ran faster, worried who would clean up all that geese poop. He was fascinated the geese had that much poop in them. Behind him, Jane had almost caught up.

The spaceship appeared among the pine trees looking like a big red rubber ball. George and Jane outpaced the smaller aliens, who became a chorus of horrible screaming against the splattering geese poop. A round hole opened in the center of the rubber ball spaceship as if it was a mouth to eat them.

George did not hesitate and dove head first inside. He landed on his belly as the yellow stone Bernard popped out of his sweaty hand. It rolled across a wavy floor toward a hole in the center of the round spaceship.

Jane stumbled inside and jumped across the wavy floor, grabbing for the yellow stone. It tumbled from her fingertips and disappeared into the dark hole.

Gina ran inside, with the other aliens stumbling in behind her. She yelled, "Get Bernard out of that hole. My sensors record it will not work. George was too contaminated with bird poop and it contaminated Bernard."

"What'll happen to Bernard?" George asked Gina.

"I don't know. But we need to get out of the spaceship. Bernard's contamination initiated the self-destruct mechanism and everything will start melting."

"Where can we go?" All the aliens sang this in perfect harmony.

"We'll live in Jane's apartment until a rescue ship arrives. I've already sent the emergency signal," Gina said.

"No, you're not moving in with me. I don't want any of you in my apartment. I only have one bedroom and there's too many of you. I want to be left alone." Jane pushed her way to the door. She tripped on the door's edge and tumbled onto the ground of pine needles.

"Everyone out," Gina yelled.

Before Jane could stand up, the aliens fell out of the door. They piled on top of her leaving Gina and George in the spaceship, which began to smell like burned rubber.

"What about me? Are you going to turn me off?" George had a worried look toward Gina.

"No, turning you off would have happened to activate Bernard, which won't happen now," Gina said. "Let's go."

A loud moan came out of the hole and out popped someone George thought looked like Sophia Loren from the same old movie channel.

"Bernard's back. Now, let's go George." Gina did not wait and jumped out the door.

Jane had just got up and said, "You seem to be in charge. Don't bring those aliens to my apartment." She wished she could have the lush eyelashes and perfect lips of this alien who was the most human looking.

"George calls me Gina, so let's stay with that. We need to get away before this spaceship melts."

As Gina ran off toward the other aliens gathered around her sedan, Jane shouted, "What about George?"

Hearing his name, George jumped out of the spaceship carrying an alien and explaining, "This is Bernard and he looks like Sophia Loren. Don't you think?"

"I don't care. Let's go," said Jane as the spaceship emitted a strong odor of geese poop.

They all gathered around Jane's sedan and watched the red rubber ball spaceship melt into a green gelatin mess. Then, it swiftly transitioned into a purple cloud that floated away.

The aliens looked at Jane with pitiful eyes.

She threw her arms in the air. "All right, you can move in with me. But don't touch my food."

"Okay, everyone. Let's go to Jane's place before the geese come back," said Gina.

"Great. You and I can be friends," George said to Jane.

"I don't need friends. I just got out of a five year relationship with a boyfriend who tortured me with his affairs. My parents were involved in my two older brothers' families and I felt like an outsider. It's enough to keep in touch on video chat every two weeks. I'm better off being alone," Jane said.

"This is why I love human's reality shows. They have so much drama," said an alien who looked like all the Kardashians together.

"George can't go to our planet. He came to life on this planet, so technically he's an Earthian," said Gina.

"Also, if he came back with us, our technicians might turn him off," the Sophia Loren looking Bernard said.

"I can be your roommate after everyone leaves," said George, smiling.

"Whoa. I was not looking for a roommate. Although, I don't want you being turned off, either. Fine, let's get out of here," Jane said.

Jane discovered the aliens could fly by holding their breath, puffing up like a balloon, and poking out a tail that acted like a propeller. If anyone saw them flying along the freeway following her brown sedan, they would have thought she was pulling along odd looking balloons. After the first day, she showed the aliens how to take the back roads to her apartment and avoid people's cell phone video taking.

For the next week, the aliens returned to the park's

administrative building. This was where they sent their "help" signal before their spaceship melted and where the rescue spaceship would come.

They told Jane their rescue spaceship would only land during daylight. So, each night they came back to Janet's apartment and slept all over the place. She didn't ask them what they ate and drank to keep alive. Some of them looked like vampires.

Jane was glad George was stuck in the "on" position and he was happy cleaning geese poop from around the Fun Fun Water Park. Jane convinced the park's administrators to hire the aliens to also keep the area clean of geese poop. None of the staff spoke about the strange little beings or why the geese did so much pooping. They were just glad these people kept the area clean of the recent abundance of geese poop.

At the end of the week one night and after everyone was asleep, Jane sat on her bed with George. He looked around to make sure no one was listening.

"I've been in contact with the rescue spaceship. It'll be here tomorrow. I told Gina, but no one else. Are you still cool with me staying with you after everyone leaves?"

"Yeah, of course. We'll continue commuting together to the park." Jane smiled. George had become more like the child she wished she had, and maybe also a good friend.

"That's great. Now, I need to bring Gina over to tell you about tomorrow's plan." George waved at Gina who stood near the bathroom door.

"I sense you two are good about living together. Now, let me tell you about Bernard. He and I are co-leaders. I loved him and I thought he was brave to turn into our fuel. Except I suspect he altered the instructions and had us put him in George's hands. He knew George would be contaminated with bird poop and Bernard would be returned to himself. Instead of being brave, he failed our mission by crashing us on this planet, then failing to make new fuel."

"Okay, so why tell me this? You're not leaving Bernard here with me," Jane said.

"Don't worry, he's coming with us," Gina said. "I told you this so you'd understand Bernard's character. I want to help the geese and give them a ride on our rescue spaceship when it arrives. He hates the geese and is convincing the others to leave them behind. We have become rivals. I need your help to get the geese onboard and save everyone."

"I'll definitely help. I don't want any alien geese left behind," Jane said. "What about your people on the rescue ship? Will they go along with this?"

"The rescue ship is on automatic and crewless. I've already talked to the geese and they are happy to hitch a ride and play along with my plan," said Gina.

"What's your plan?" Jane was worried.

"I'll let you know when I have it," Gina said.

The rescue spaceship drifted out of an overcast, gray sky. With the threat of a hurricane, the park was closed and the few administrative people sheltered inside the building.

The spaceship looked like a teardrop and its dull green color blended with the gray weather. It landed in the parking lot not far from where the other spaceship used to be. Gina had gathered the aliens around the Fun Fun Water Park sign waiting for the engines to turn off. Overhead, the geese circled.

"The geese are going to steal our spaceship. Everybody run for it," yelled Bernard, shaking his fists at the geese.

The geese landed between the spaceship and the aliens. No

one had weapons, leaving the confrontation to degenerate into a lot of yelling and flailing of arms and wings. George ran in circles between the two groups yelling for everyone to stop yelling as Gina slipped into the rescue ship. Jane followed her out of curiosity.

The inside seemed bigger than the outside. The wall, ceiling, and floor were a pastel baby pink, pale blue, and a dark shade of lavender. A lemon yellow stripe traveled through the colors. A soft light illuminated a scattering of gray bean bags. Jane could not see any controls.

"Can you fly this thing?" Jane watched Gina running around looking for the anything and tripping over the bean bags.

"Of course not. I just want to turn the engines on. Ah, here's the start button."

Jane watched Gina push a white button that said 'do not push.' The spaceship trembled and it sounded like someone was pissing. Outside, the yelling and shouting stopped and, through the doorway, Jane could see everyone staring at the spaceship.

Gina went to the door and shouted, "Everyone, get on this spaceship or I'm going to take off and leave all of you behind. Bernard, everyone including the geese are getting on this spaceship."

"The geese will steal everything. They're not like us. They're different," Bernard yelled.

"No, they want to leave this planet just like us." Gina turned to Jane, "No offense, but this is not our home."

"I get it," Jane replied. "I'd like for all of you to leave, too."

"Bernard, everyone in the universe is different. That makes us all unique, diverse, and special. It keeps life alive."

"I'm afraid of them. They pooped on us," Bernard said.

"They're sorry for that. They were thinking like you are now and were scared. We do not need to be scared of each other. We all want to go home," Gina said.

A clap of thunder shook the air. The aliens and geese cared only about getting out of the thunder storm. Jane jumped off the spaceship as everyone ran past her to get on. Gina kept the engines running on idle as the last of the aliens and geese clambering aboard. Except for Bernard who stood outside the door. The first pellets of rain splattered down on him.

"You don't need me," Bernard said.

"You're the pilot. We need you. I need you," Gina said, holding out her hand for him to take.

"I'm sorry for getting scared on this planet and tricking everyone. I didn't want to die," Bernard said.

"I understand. I really like you and I want to start over. After we drop everyone off, why can take a trip to the Zippio planet. They have the most beautiful waterfalls in that section of the galactic arm."

Bernard reached out and took Gina's hands. He ducked into the spaceship as Jane and George ran through the pouring rain to her sedan.

After a month on Earth, George felt more human. The Fun Fun Water Park made him a staff member of the maintenance crew and he became a celebrity to visitors of the park. Everyone enjoyed being welcomed by his happiness.

Jane considered George as a third brother. She included him in her family's video chats and did not discourage them from thinking George was her gay friend. One day they would all meet, she promised George.

Four months later, Gina and Bernard came back and met George and Jane in their apartment. They all hugged.

"I'm so glad you're here. We've missed you two," Jane said.

"We've got a lot to tell both of you," Bernard said.

They sat at the kitchen table over glasses of iced water with watermelon slices and a squirt of spicy ketchup. Gina and Bernard excitedly announced they were buying the Fun Fun Water Park.

"The park has financial trouble and many people from our planet are coming to help," said Bernard.

"We think our people will add a little flare of excitement and fun to the park. A lot of the geese are coming to help, too," said Gina.

Jane smiled. "This will be great. But people may get scared seeing your people as they are."

"Humans will think we're wearing costumes. We'll have a souvenir shop with the same outfits for kids and adults," said Bernard, who still looked like Sophia Loren.

"Yeah, I think it'll work. Except my dad will figure you out and I know he'll be cool with it. He always believed in aliens. He'll be excited to meet everyone," Jane said.

"When do you start?" George had the broadest smile.

"Tomorrow. The spaceship is landing at the center of the park and will stay there as an attraction. Plus, we plan to get the geese spaceship out of the administrative building and put it next to our spaceship," said Gina.

"Let's celebrate with another squirt of spice ketchup," George said.

A year later and with the success of the water park, Gina and Bernard were offered to franchise to other locations. They said no. They didn't want it to feel like an alien invasion.

Human Pollution, Invasive Species, and a Planet Saved

The five human space travelers were worn out when they climbed down from their landing craft onto the habitable planet swinging around a double sun system. Their spaceship reached almost the speed of light, which was still not fast enough for five people with competing opinions to be stuck on a cramped spaceship. On landing, Barney was amazed they didn't kill each other along the way.

The planet was half a light year from Earth and had remained hidden from prying Earthian eyes by dark matter. New technology revealed that the matter was not dark, but too bright to give off heat. When the planet was discovered, it was too similar to Earth not to visit.

Before they launched, company executives from a diverse group of wealthy industries ignored public opinion, who wanted to prevent humans from contaminating the planet. The louder, aggressive opinions of individuals with a lot of money demanded conquest of the planet for its possible mineral wealth.

A quick consortium formed calling themselves It's About Us and they were the first to launch. Barney thought the investors should have spent more time assessing the crew's personalities than being the first onto an unknown planet. He wondered about his own motivation for coming on the trip. For this mission, few people volunteered, worried about the hurried construction of the spaceship.

The mission was to help him forget the overdose death of his teenage son two years before. His wife blamed herself as she walked out to live with her sister by the ocean and start over. He blamed himself and volunteered to get off Earth as soon as possible. The only people who volunteered turned out to be running from something, too.

Standing beside their landing craft, the five space travelers glanced through their helmet visors at a pale purple sky and twin yellow suns. Except their focus was quickly drawn to their feet where they stared in stunned silence at thick brown stems as high as their knees topped with thin round, fragile petals.

The petals presented themselves to the human aliens with shockingly varying hues of pure yellow, green, red, blue, and all the shades between. Some of the flowers melded into a patchwork of perfect orange, brown, and gray. Some petals had a tint of black, while others possessed white for agreement. Barney thought the dazzling colors made their bland silver landing craft and their colorless spacesuits look blander.

Hoober had walked several feet to stand among the

flowers. Except he was looking up at the two suns. Everyone else stayed close to the lander's door looking at the flowers and Hoober.

"What do you think the flowers smell like?" Hoober used his outside speaker that the others heard with their helmet receivers. Barney was suspicious about why Hoober did not use the helmet to helmet comms which were recorded.

"Do you really care what the flowers smell like?" Barney said through his outside speakers, just in case. He worried that Hoober, who was neither the youngest nor the oldest of the crew, would do something rebellious against Space Mission Admin who was their contact with Earth.

Before the trip, they shamed Hoober for having a large belly that barely passed the flight requirements. Also, they did not pack any of Hoober's spicy, fatty foods he wanted to eat at landing in honor of his Thai father and German mother. Barney nor the other crew defended Hoober, which made Barney nervous about what Hoober would do among the beautiful flowers.

"Our instruments and sensors don't detect an odor. They do detect more colors than what we're seeing," said Barney, switching to internal communications. Being four decades old, on the long trip he told stories about when he was happy growing up in Japan. Some of the flowers reminded him of where he grew up.

"I don't believe that. These flowers are so beautiful, they must smell fantastic. My parents, if they were alive, would have had a family Chinese proverb to say about them," said Peggy through her outside speakers.

Barney wished Peggy liked him more. They were the oldest with she only a year older. He thought they should have more in common.

She looked toward a range of gray mountains along the horizon. "We're in a wide valley and those mountains have foliage on them, but not like these flowers."

"I don't care about the mountains. I want to cry looking at all these beautiful colorful flowers," said Clarinet, using her outside speakers like Hoober.

Barney envied her youth. She was a quarter of a century old and from the generation whose parents named their children after musical instruments. She told him on the trip how her parents never taught her how to play the clarinet and she never felt real. She wanted to take this trip so her parents would treat her as a real adult. Barney had no answer in response and she stopped talking to him.

The visor did not hide the tears on her pale face. "I'm in love with these fragile bright flowers."

"I've seen old photos of flowers on Earth and they used to be this colorful. Now, our flowers are dull from useless opinions," Trumpet said, also through his speakers.

Barney was getting more worried with no one using their helmet to helmet comms. He spied Trumpet turn his blue eyes toward Clarinet. Yet, her visor and hazel eyes faced the flowers. Barney had grown tired of listening to Trumpet's frustration at trying to be romantic with Clarinet. Or how he came on this mission so he could claim hero status and prove to his dad he could be someone important.

"We need to be cautious and keep our spacesuits on even though the atmosphere is breathable. Space Mission Admin warned about spores hanging in the air." Barney used his helmet communications.

"I don't think Earth flowers were ever this brilliant," said Peggy, through her speakers. She bent down and caressed a petal standing out from one of the brown stems. It moved with the touch of her hand, but not by the unmoving air.

Barney got frustrated that everyone had turned off their helmet to helmet comms and were only using their outside speakers.

"I hope the flowers don't smell like orange. I hate orange," Hoober said. He was looking at the mud on his shoes and not the flowers.

"Why do you hate orange?" Clarinet inched closer to Hoober.

"My father used an orange paddle on me when I failed a school test. Sometimes I failed a test just to get hit by him so I could hate him more."

"Could these flowers love us? I always hoped love would win." Clarinet took a few more steps from the lander, careful not to step on a flower. She inched closer to Hoober, who was six or eight feet away.

"Save us from what? Humanity is content as a dull, violent species. These flowers show how unbeautiful we are as a species," said Trumpet. He stayed a few steps behind Clarinet, as if not wanting to get too close to the weird flowers.

Clarinet said, "We could bring some of these flowers to Earth and let people decide whether or not they could save us. Except, I don't know what flowers to take. They're all so beautiful."

"I don't want to share our spaceship with these crazy flowers. They belong here on this planet. If we take them to Earth, they may change our opinions about ourselves," said Trumpet.

"No, we definitely are not bringing alien life to Earth. It's against Space Mission Admin protocol," said Barney. He watched Hoober lift his shoe to peel off a crushed flower from his sole.

"This is why one of us should be in charge. We can't rely on those knuckleheads on Earth who were hired by those nitwits of It's About Us to make decisions. Besides, we're not even in communication with them until our command orbiter circles around again and reestablishes comms," Peggy said, looking at the mountains more than the flowers at her feet.

"Why do we need to tell Space Mission Admin what we're seeing? Maybe we should just take off our helmets and lie down among the flowers," said Clarinet. "I took this trip to find love. My ex husband hit me whenever he wanted and I wanted to get far away from him. These flowers might be my great escape."

"Yeah, why do we need to listen to Space Mission Admin tell us what to do? We can do whatever we want," said Hoober.

Barney wanted to do something. The painful memory of their arguments and strong opinions on the trip to this flower planet was still too vivid. He worried they would rather stay than make the trip back. Barney had his doubts about making the trip back, too.

Before any of them could move or say anything, Hoober snapped off his helmet and threw it toward the hatchway. He clumped down cross-legged among the flowers and took a deep breath from whatever fragrance came off the flowers he crushed when sitting

"These flowers are making me love myself," they heard Hoober say from their outside receivers.

"You can't get back on the spaceship. You're contaminated," Barney screamed through his speakers so Hoober could hear. He wondered if his voice was heard among the beautiful flowers.

"Leave him alone. Let's see if the dunderhead dies," said Trumpet through his outside speakers, loud enough so Hoober and everyone heard him.

"How are we going to explain this to Space Mission Admin?" Barney thought leaving Hoober behind would be great. They would be free of his stupid pranks. Barney had been bullied most of his life, driving him to detest pranksters.

"Since I'm still alive, I'm going to be an alien flower." Hoober laughed.

"How are you feeling?" Clarinet asked. "If you live, I want to love you forever." This last part was a whisper only Barney heard since he stood nearby.

"He's looking bad. Aren't you, Hoober? Are you going to die?" Trumpet sounded jealous that Clarinet was giving Hoober attention.

"I feel great. I love these flowers. I feel them loving me, too," said Hoober. He lifted his brownish face toward the double suns to enjoy the rays.

"Get up and put your helmet back on. We can still decontaminate you," Barney yelled through his outside speakers.

"You can't order him to do anything," said Peggy. "That's Space Mission Admin's responsibility. My dad and my ex always yelled at me to do what they said. I hate yelling."

"In a few more minutes our spaceship will complete orbit and restore Earth communications," said Clarinet. She took a few steps toward Hoober.

"Fine, Hoober can sit there until he turns into one of those flowers or sinks into that orange mud," said Trumpet.

"This is all against protocol," Barney said. He wished he had the rule book on his tablet to show everyone on their display. Although, he worried this situation may not be in any rule set by Space Mission Admin.

"I can hear everyone through your speakers and I don't care. I want to stay with the flowers. They're my new family," Hoober said, allowing a few tears to fall on some of the petals. "I didn't smell anything before. But now I can smell sweet honeysuckle, which was my safe place as a kid when I needed to hide from my father."

"I feel so bad for you. I won't leave you here," said Clarinet, moving next to Hoober.

"We have to leave him here. Something is infecting him. Where are the insects to pollinate these flowers? How do they reproduce? Is Hoober becoming a flower?" Barney stood next to the hatchway realizing there had been no wind since they arrived. Without wind or insects, he wanted to know how the flowers pollinated.

"Stop crying. I hate seeing men cry. The survey of this planet found no carbon-based life. Nothing here should exist. What else have we missed?" Peggy searched the area and saw flowers all the way to the mountains.

"What forms of life can they be? Maybe we should take them back to Earth. We'll introduce them to the executives of that stupid company It's About Us. We can watch what happens to those idiots," Trumpet said. He stared at Clarinet who focused her attention on Hoober.

"Maybe Hoober has something by sitting with the flowers," said Clarinet.

"No, everybody needs to get back into the landing craft," Barney shouted.

"You're not Space Mission Admin. You can't order us to do stuff, even if you are old," said Clarinet. "I want to be with the flowers like Hoober. I feel them calling me."

The three watched in shock as Clarinet lifted off her helmet and tossed it near the hatchway next to Hoober's. Her reddish hair danced across her shoulders as if happy to be free of the helmet. She found a spot next to Hoober, brushed back the flowers, and sat on the bare orange ground in a lotus position.

"What are you smelling?" Trumpet took a step toward Clarinet, as if wanting to save her.

Clarinet gagged and put her hand over her mouth to resist throwing up. She held her other hand in the air for everyone to wait. After less than a minute, when even Barney wondered if she would run back for her helmet, she threw her other hand in the air.

"I can smell roses and not some rot that I smelled at first. Roses are my favorite favorite smell. They remind me of my mom," said Clarinet.

Trumpet stomped his feet in a tantrum, kicking some of the flowers over. He looked at the hatchway, which was his way home, and at Clarinet sitting beside Hoober. Finally, he yanked off his helmet and hurled it toward the other two helmets by the hatchway. He had a scowl on his pale face as he shoved himself between the two. Trumpet sat on several flowers. "Did you fart?" he asked Hoober.

"You three are jeopardizing the mission. You should have waited for Space Mission Admin to tell us what to do. Now you're all contaminated," shouted Barney through his speakers.

"How do you know we're contaminated? I feel like the person I should have been," Hoober said.

"I like the smell of farts," Trumpet whispered to Hoober.

"Trumpet, you're the pilot. I don't care if you're contaminated or not. Put your helmet back on and let's get out of here," Peggy said through her speaker.

"I can fly the spaceship back to Earth," said Barney.

"You don't even know how to start the engines. We need Trumpet," Peggy said.

"We need everyone. Hoober knows the engineering to run the engines and Clarinet manages communication and guidance," said Barney.

"Then, the ones not needed are you and me," Peggy told Barney. "The two with helmets on and not sitting with the flowers."

Barney's biggest fear had been that his administrator coordinator position was beyond insignificant and could save no one, not even himself.

"I'm the AI coordinator and I think the AI hid these flowers from us and landed us here so the AI could take over the spaceship." She communicated helmet to helmet with Barney.

Barney watched the three sitting among the dazzlingly colorful flowers and not talking. "There have to be spores in the air making them complacent like that."

"Look around. There's nothing floating in the air," Peggy said.

"The air could be filled with spores in a wavelength we can't see. We need to get control of this situation." To control his anxiety, Barney needed to do something. He arranged the discarded helmets in a row just inside the landing craft's hatchway. Standing back, he felt at ease with the helmets in a neat, straight line. They provided the order he needed for the confusing situation he was in.

"I can't go back to Earth," Peggy told Barney through their helmets.

"Why not?" He faced her.

"I never liked my life. While growing up, my parents and teachers ridiculed my ambition to go into space. Then I lived through a bad marriage and pointless relationships afterward.

For the first time in my life, looking at these flowers makes me feel better about myself."

Peggy took off her helmet and placed it next to the other three. She shook her thick black hair to loosen the curls and faced the distant mountains.

She did not sit with the three, but sat next to the landing craft on sandy soil scorched of flowers from the thrust of the engines when they landed. "I feel achy and there's a sickening sweet vanilla smell that my mom smelled like when she died. Now, I smell a campfire when I was ten and she was with me."

Barney turned to Peggy so only she would hear through his outside speakers, "Do you think the flowers are intelligent life on this planet?"

She said to Barney's helmet receiver, "I already figured that the flowers could be controlling us, but I don't care. It's better than being controlled by the spaceship's AI or Space Mission Admin or It's About Us company executives."

"There's no food and water here, unless we become like the flowers and survive on what they feed on. I don't know what that is. We might stop being human if we survive on the produce of this planet." Barney wanted to cry for not knowing what to do. He knew Peggy hated crying men.

Hoober, Clarinet, and Trumpet sat silently with their backs to Peggy, who sat in a cross legged position ignoring the three ignoring her. Barney stood by the hatchway ignoring the flowers. He worried they would lure him to stay like they did with the others.

A shrill sound erupted from the landing craft as communication was re-established with Space Mission Admin. A dense male AI voice shouted from the speakers of the discarded helmets, yet Barney doubted anyone cared to listen.

He turned down his volume to tame the shouting of Space

Mission Admin feeding headline news. The media paid for most of the mission and took priority over asking about the safety of the space travelers.

For international news, he heard about another religious war, a territorial conflict over a useless desolate area, and two civil wars between sparring egos. For U.S. news, he listened to a mass shooting in an elementary school. The shooter used a new gun approved by the NRA to deliver multiple kills in record time. After the shooting, manufacturers of the gun and ammunition suppliers celebrated record sales and profits.

Barney stared at Peggy who stared back. She looked away, staring at the mountains in the distance. The other three seemed at peace among the flowers.

"Maybe I need to take some of these flowers back to Earth. They could save us from our opinions and lead us from our tragedies," Barney said through his speakers.

"If they are intelligent life, like I think they are, you can't *take* the flowers. That would be like kidnapping. Let them decide if they want to go or not," Peggy kept staring at the distant mountains as if they were calling her.

Barney cautiously stepped away from the landing craft where the flowers kept changing colors every few seconds as if waving to him. He was careful not to step on any of them. As he bent down to look closer, a bunch of them leaped out of the orange soil and onto his gloved hands.

Stumbling back, he screamed trying to shake the flowers off his gloves. They wouldn't come off as he ran to the hatchway. He scraped his gloves between two of the helmets to get the flowers off. Both gloves popped off inside the landing craft with the flowers still hanging on to them. A few more flowers that had clung to his arms, torso, and legs jumped inside the landing craft, too.

Staring at his bare hands in the warm air, Barney realized he was exposed. Peggy came over and helped him take off his helmet. She placed it neatly beside the others inside the hatchway.

Barney took a deep breath and smelled the same odor as when he found his son's body. Barney shivered from the memory.

"The first smell is bad, yet the second is good," said Peggy.

Barney sniffed the air and smelled the sharp sweet aroma of a fresh pine tree. It reminded him of the pine forest where he used to walk in better days with his son.

They spun around at a loud snap and stared in horror as the hatchway sealed shut. Barney ran up and pounded his fists on the hatchway as he heard the engines turn on.

"With the helmets inside, the ship's AI thinks we're onboard. It's going to launch," Peggy dragged Barney away. All five ran from the landing craft as the thrusters burned away more flowers.

Watching the landing craft sail away into the purple sky between double suns, Barney wondered if the flowers had launched the landing craft.

Despite having two suns, day and night closely matched Earth's. During the day, the flowers emitted a jelly-like moisture that satisfied the humans' thirst and hunger. They even bathed in it. The flowers did now know how to tell them it was their poop and pee.

At night, the flowers placed soft petals on the orange ground for the five humans to sleep on. They did not notice how the flowers leaped out of the ground to hug each other in their method of pollination.

On the third morning, the dramatic opinionated

argument between Hoober, Trumpet, and Clarinet mesmerized the flowers like a soap opera. Barney and Peggy had enough of them and walked to the mountains where they hoped one day to save the flowers from human opinions.

By early afternoon, they stood at the base of the mountain range that was covered in thick tall red trees with yellow leaves that looked like flower petals. They followed paths between the trees leading to larger petals holding clear water and soft brown balls that tasted like candy. Peggy and Barney felt welcomed.

The flowers docked the landing craft with the command orbiter, easily overcame the AI, and made improvements to the propulsion system to go faster than light speed. On Earth, they used the helmets to land the spaceship without being destroyed by Space Mission Admin, who would have considered them an alien invasion.

The flowers went to work saving humanity from their opinions.

Alien Hope

Leaning On an Alien Harvester

"I saw you stealing glances at me. What do you want?" Lucy snapped at a man standing next to her on a concrete train station platform.

Designed to hold masses of commuters, only a smattering of travelers waited for the train as a chilly wind whipped into Lucy's reddish face. The cold did not appear to bother the man's bald brown head.

"I want to get away from you. I have guilts in my life that haunt me." His voice sounded hollow.

He had a hint of gray in his eyes as he stared at the steel tracks before them. He looked like the other commuters standing around waiting for a train to take them home. Lucy was suspicious. She saw no one staring at their electronic devices, reading a book, or falling asleep while standing up.

"Your guilts have nothing to do with me. Don't hang around me when we get on this train. I don't want you near me," Lucy said.

"I don't have a choice. I'm getting on this train because of you."

He sounded whiny with a shrill sad voice as if he was used to people not listening to him. Lucy hated whiny people. She looked around at the other commuters and wondered what was wrong with them. They stood staring at the steel tracks as if they didn't belong there. As if they wanted to exist in some other time and place. The bald man spoke again.

"I was on this train before and introduced myself as Henry to a woman sitting in the aisle seat next to me. I told her about my guilts, hoping that confessing to her would free me from the commute. Yet, she already knew my guilts, which she used to keep me on the train."

Lucy hated this Henry person. He made her feel as if he knew something she should know, too. She was grateful to hear the short toot-toot of the commuter train coming around a bend in the tracks. The smattering of commuters inched closer to her as commuters do, anxious to be the first to funnel through the double doors and escape the waiting. Lucy stood where she was and the others did not keep their distance. She felt like her presence drew them closer to her and it made her feel strong.

"I don't know who you are," Lucy said to Henry.

"You're that woman I confessed my guilts to."

Lucy stared at the man's round face. He had a long, straight nose and laugh lines at the corners of his brown eyes. He did not seem like a person who laughed. At least not anymore.

"That wasn't me. I've never seen you before," Lucy said.

She wanted to say more, but the roar of the approaching diesel engine prevented it. When the train stopped, Lucy noted there were only two cars. She thought there should have been more.

The annoying man got in front of her and boarded the

train. Lucy stood there aggravated as other men and a few women, all taller, pushed in front of her. Her aggravation became frustration and she stomped up the metal stairs as the last passenger.

She spied Henry sitting by himself in a window seat. Although there were other places to sit, Lucy was drawn to sitting next to him in the aisle seat. She had to know more about what he was saying.

"Maybe I just look like this other woman."

"You don't look like her now. You're short and she was tall. You have blond hair and reddish skin. She had brown hair and pale skin. She had blue eyes and yours is green."

"You're crazy." Lucy stood up to find another seat, but none were available. She considered going to the other train car, but she did not and sat back down.

"It'll come back to you," Henry said.

"What'll come back to me?"

"The memory of who you are. When I told you my guilts, I felt liberated and this gave me strength to escape from you. I got off at the train station where we were standing. You came to get me and I realized then you were an alien from another planet." Henry stared into the back of the seat before him. It had a small pocket that should have held a train ticket, but did not.

"That's crap. I'm not an alien and I've never seen you before now."

"When you got off to bring me back, the other passengers you held on this train escaped, too. You feed off our negative energy to continue your existence. You became desperate when we got off. Bringing the train back and picking us up made you weak. You forgot who you were."

"I know who I am. I always know who I am."

Lucy could not remember who she was as the train picked up speed. Henry stopped talking and she used the silence to remember more. She saw a few empty seats.

When did the train make stops? She tried to remember what her train stop was. Glancing beside her, Henry stared out the window as if wanting to be elsewhere. He looked sad.

Frightened by her lack of memory, Lucy stomped into the next train car, where the smell of sweat and rebreathed human air surfaced into her opened eyes. She sat in the first empty seat by a window. Night had fallen. She remembered it was daylight when she got on a few minutes ago. Lucy wondered if she had fallen asleep. She focused on her reflection in the train window.

What she saw in her reflection was colorless. She could not see the green in her eyes or the blond in her hair. Without color, her hair could have been brown and her eyes blue. She thought about the stranger and what he said. I have to be strong when talking to that Henry guy again. I need to tell him I have prestige and authority over my life.

She missed talking to him.

No, Lucy decided. She needed to be away from his body and smell. She leaned her head back and let herself move in tempo with the train's rocking motion as it carried her further down the steel tracks. She drifted into a dream of living in another solar system.

Lucy existed there in a semi-cybernated state. She was tall with brown hair, pale skin, and blue eyes. She controlled her aged spacecraft as it carried commuters to landing stations between planets and moons of that solar system.

In this dream, she adored the grand Sun drifting past her portal on each trip. It was a mass of power and strength burning in the coldness of space. Until it exploded into a brilliant flash.

Her derelict spaceship drifted out among the residue of the Sun's burned plasma. Space traveling commuters onboard yelled for help. In this dream, she only wanted to save herself. Lucy left them drifting in the starry ashes as she escaped in a pod toward a blue planet with too much water for her liking. At least it had commuter trains that looked like her spaceship.

The train jolted to a stop, waking Lucy and leaving her regretting she was no longer living that interstellar life. She wanted to go back there, transporting commuters between planets and moons in a solar system where she felt at home. Foggy from her sleep, Lucy ran off the train thinking it was her stop.

"I'm going home," she told herself as she descended the metal stairs. On the concrete platform, she realized this was not her stop.

She did not know what her stop looked like, but this barren, concrete platform lacked a feeling of home. She heard voices that sounded hollow, like an empty echo. They became distant, which worried her. Where were they going? She saw no one getting off.

Immersed in confusion, Lucy got back on the train before the doors chimed closed. Climbing the metal stairs gave her a feeling of loss, as if something got off when she got on.

Lucy found the train car where Henry continued sitting by the window. She sat next to him and said, "Look at me."

With his closed eyes, he said, "No."

Lucy stared at the other commuters, who stared into the back of the seat before them. They each turned to look at her and they looked away and she looked away. There were so few of them left.

She looked up and down the train car for the conductor to ask when the next scheduled stop was, yet there was no conductor. Lucy told the eyes closed Henry, "Open your eyes and look at me."

He did not. Instead, Henry said, "After I came back on this train, I found out how to escape from you forever. I told the others. When you stepped off the train this time, many went to where they should go. Except the ones who are the saddest. They fear who they will meet in their afterlife if they detrain. I don't know how long they'll stay on this train keeping you company and giving you strength."

"Nobody is leaving me." Lucy was not sure why, but Henry was helping her come back from some mental fatigue. She struggled to sort through what her thoughts were before she forgot them. Quickly, Lucy remembered this commuter train was her escape pod. Coming to this watery planet, she changed from who she used to be.

Henry cleared his throat. "I made a mistake and lost my way. I wanted to find home, but I was troubled by my guilts. You lured me here by telling me your guilts of abandoning your commuters."

"It was your suicide that brought you here, not me. It is your guilt forcing you to stay with me." Lucy remembered everything as she watched the small man become grayer. She grew angry with him.

"After my daughter graduated college, I admitted to her and my wife that I had always been gay. I could not handle their rejection. That is my truth. When you got off the train to capture me, you grew weak and I sensed what was your truth. I learned how you used to be a commuter who commuted so much you became the vehicle of your commute. Your self and soul merged reluctantly with the cyber machine of the commuting spaceship," said Henry, keeping his eyes closed.

"Stop talking about what I was. I never wanted to be that person taking commuters to places I wanted to visit. I could not get off that commute and that nova gave me the opportunity to escape and be free." Who she was in that other solar system became clear in Lucy's head with a vengeance.

"I was only a common transport taking passengers to their moons and planets. No one paid me any attention. Here, I am free to do what I want." Lucy felt happier admitting this.

"You're not free. You are still trapped in a commute, except now you are going to places that do not exist."

"That's crap. I saved myself from commuting."

"You left out of fear and now you have guilts about leaving your commuters without a commute," said Henry.

"They're dead," Lucy said.

"You are dead."

"I'm alive. I have to be. I don't want to die."

The train sped up, racing down the steel tracks as if curves and switch tracks were just being invented. Lucy envisioned the train as a ghost running from station to station where the living felt only a wisp of stale air curl around their faces. She looked around at no more commuters. Even the most desperate found their way home.

Lucy stifled a rising fear that the train car looked like a metal coffin. She wanted to be strong. "Where is everyone? I didn't feel this train stop."

Henry continued with a soft, trembling voice. "You don't realize you are two people. It was your soul that walked off this train trying to find your death. Your cyber side brought you back to continue the commute."

"That's wrong. It wasn't my stop."

"Exactly."

Lucy stood. "You're trapped here like me with all your guilts. You're never leaving me."

Henry broke open his eyes. They had a vacant distant look. "When you got off this train, I faced my guilts. The others did the same, which is how they eventually left."

"But you're still on this train," Lucy said. She had confidence she was still in control.

"I was the only human on this train, which is why we are talking. The others were the commuters who were on your transport when the nova hit. You used their guilts as energy and brought them here. I'm here to save you," said Henry.

"I don't need saving. This is my home."

"Except you cannot be a commute without commuters."

"I can be whoever I want. I demand that you stay here with me." Lucy felt as if she was fading away.

"My soul has already left. It's time for you to stop commuting and go home, too. Don't worry. It'll be a happy place with the friends and family you had before you began commuting."

In The Beginning

"I ain't reading that book you got in front of me. Whoever you are, I ain't letting you corrupt my mind with no filthy propaganda."

Harley remained tied down in the most comfortable chair he ever sat in. Almost as if the chair was made for his thin body. Although his arms were glued to the arm rests and his legs to the leg rests, the velvety material and soft cushions felt as if he was floating on air. He tried not to enjoy the comfort since he was tied down.

There were no ties he could see, yet any struggle to free himself left him in the same position. He scanned the floor for any evidence of his bindings. It was a hard, dark grayish material.

To his left and right, coarse gray blocks arched around him to form what he assumed was a tight roundhouse. The chair's high back and his confinement prevented him from turning around to confirm this.

Looking up, he saw a concrete ledge and above that a gray

overcast sky showing no details of what was beyond. He couldn't help but relax to the flow of cool air around him and the sweet aroma of honeysuckle flowers, his favorite smell.

Before Harley was an opened book with purple binding on top of a yellow pedestal. Glossy black lettering across pearl white paper made the words easy to read. Harley hated all of it.

He felt detached from some period of time, as if ghostly angels had tried pulling his callused hands up while ragged demons tugged down at his blistered feet. He thought about purgatory, a place between love and shadows.

Harley shook this thought out of his head. He wanted to know how he got into the comfortable chair and how long he had been facing the pedestal and the book. Even more important, he wanted to know who put him here. He was not scared.

"Who are you? Where are you? Show yourself. I ain't reading your book 'cause it's got nothin' but your lies."

Harley did not know this. He did not know what the book was about. Only that he did not like being forced to do anything. Particularly reading, which was his worst subject in high school and one of the reasons he dropped out. He thought about how to escape, except he did not know where he would go since he did not know where he was.

"I'm not scared," Harley shouted at the book.

He remembered pieces of his life as a bricklayer where being scared was not allowed among husky men. Except, he got scared when he thought about how useless his life had become with all the drinking and living in a dingy apartment, alone. At twenty-five, he wished he had done more to feel better about himself.

In his life, liquor helped satisfy his fears. When it was not enough, Harley ducked behind street drugs. Coming out of the high, the drugs got him more scared after having no memory of why he had been scared or what drugs he took to not be scared. Leaning back in the chair, Harley hated remembering all this. He could take a nap in the chair.

He jerked forward, yelling, "Who wants me to read that book? Show yourself." Harley wanted to be on a job site where the work pulled at his muscle and he could be fearless against what scared him.

A scratching noise startled him and made him look up at the concrete ledge. Harley spied somebody crawling on the ledge above him.

"Hey, you up there. Let me go." Harley twisted in his chair, trying to free himself until he heard a low growl come from the thing on the ledge. A chill of terror shook through him. He looked away toward the book that was tilted enough for him to read the large print.

Knowledge is not destroyed nor created.
It always existed.

Harley pushed his eyes shut, soaking in the darkness. "Damn you, I'm not reading no more. Your stupid book can just sit there. I'm not reading any of it."

He tightened his fists and remembering the last time he read a book. He was a pudgy kid in tenth grade when the teacher made him read Bram Stoker's *Dracula.* His classmates and the teacher ridiculed him for being frightened of the book.

During that year, every day he walked off the school bus and slipped into the small apartment to wait for his mother to come home from waitressing. He sat on the couch and kept his feet off the floor with his knees to his chin so no imaginary monsters would grab his feet.

The crackerbox apartment got darker until he had every light on to ward off the blackness and any vampires lurking in the shadows. When his mother got home, she yelled at him for wasting money on lights. She turned off most of them before fixing something to eat.

Harley wanted to be a hero to himself, yet he continued to fear the lack of light and closed spaces. His mother didn't care. She was happy when he stopped going to school and got a construction job to help pay the rent. In the comfortable, confining chair, Harley wondered if one of those monsters he imagined was on the ledge above him.

He kept his eyes closed, worried about what he was not seeing. I've got to stop this nonsense, he thought. There are no monsters from my childhood staring at me with talons, ready to pounce.

Harley heard a scratch like a talon scraping along the concrete ledge. He opened his eyes, but was too afraid to look up. He watched the book flip to the next page as if by a slight breeze.

In the beginning,
Knowledge lived as a singularity,
a point within
the Pure Energy of existence.

Harley looked up at the scraping sound to avoid reading anymore of the nonsense. Even without being tied down, he was frozen with fright.

The monster had long curled talons and thick black hairs over its head and body, leaving its pale face exposed. The monster's tapered ears rose high over its sloping skull and a wide mouth revealed two rows of pointed green teeth. It stared down at Harley with coal black eyes.

An instant fear gripped him as Harley watched the

monster's long black talons raise its stout body as if ready to pounce. He could not watch. Another page flipped over.

The singularity burst into controlled chaos and
blossomed into stable worlds.
The Pure Energy lifted Knowledge
into life vessels on those worlds.

"Aaah! I ain't reading no more." Harley looked up to see if the monster heard him.

The hideous creature pulled a long pink tongue across its thick red lips. Harley did not dare close his eyes again. There were other monsters from his childhood he worried could become real. He struggled to free himself, yet could not feel his bindings. He had to look away and was drawn again to the flipping of another page.

Knowledge brought love
And life adapted
to mortality and disorder.

Harley wanted to know who was turning the pages. He wondered if it was the monster. He hated choosing between the monster and the book. "Damn it. Hey, you up there. You wanna eat me, then go ahead. Come on, jump down and get me. I can't do nothin' about it."

The monster glared at Harley with narrowing eyes and a deeply bent, hairy brow. He stared at the monster with clenched teeth until his jaw hurt. The pain felt good. It made him believe he was alive and could stand against the monster's glare. For no reason, Harley experienced a sudden clarity in his thoughts of where he had been before the comfortable, confining chair.

He remembered torn leather seating, shabby curtains, and rough stains on a bar counter where he drank his beer and rye whiskey alone. With his deep earthy skin, he felt as if he was melting into the brown and dark of the bar scene. He was thinking of finding a less crowded place when the bar filled with light.

It was an artificial light Harley did not think belonged to anything made on Earth. Something happened before the light that he could not remember. Instead, he found himself floating outside toward a hovering, cigar-shaped object.

"That's it. You're a monster alien from another planet and you've abducted me onto your spaceship. What're you gonna do with me? You gonna poke me with needles or shove something down my throat or up my ass? I'll fight you, even if you got me tied down. Let me go, now."

Harley stared at the monster and thought it looked something like him, maybe in the eyes. *That's not true. I may be a bad person, but I'm not a monster,* he believed.

The creature on the ledge gave a low, deep throated gurgle that ended with thick drool hanging off its lips. With a jerk, it straightened up and howled, causing Harley to shiver with fright. He refused to close his eyes. He did not want to look at the monster anymore. That left the book and another flip of a page.

As the universe expanded
and on only the most beautiful worlds,
life vessels abandoned love.

"Stop it. You're putting things in my head I don't want. I won't let you poison me with your alien ideas. I won't. You hear me, monster? You hear what I'm saying to you?"

Harley had frightening images of yelling at his last girl-friend, who wanted to love him. But love scared him. He did not want to love someone who could turn out to be like his mother. Or worse, like his father, who left when Harley was nine.

He had to look away from the ugly creature. Harley could not tell how many pages were left to flip. He wanted to know what would happen when he came to the last page. He stared at another page flipping over.

The loveless lives
formed clear lines of separation
from the Knowledge.

Harley flexed the muscles in his arms and legs, trying to move. He did not want to close his eyes again and find more surprises when he opened them. He did not want to read the book because the words seemed to make sense. Harley took his chances looking at the monster. It was the most immediate danger, anyway. The book wasn't going anywhere and neither am I, he thought.

The creature repositioned itself with its hairy back to Har-ley, watching something on the other side of the wall. Harley worried there were more monsters coming. He looked away. The flipping of another page made him want to scream in frustration.

Seeking their own Knowledge,
those with no love
found anti-Knowledge.

"Hey, monster. Why'd you want me reading your damn book, anyway? It has nothin' to do with me." Harley stared at the monster's back and worried about what it was looking at.

He could not control his fear that something worse was coming.

"Someone help me. Help!" Harley screamed in anger. He fought frantically with his comfortable bindings. He was out of breath when he finally stopped. With nothing else to do, he looked at the book for answers and waited as another page flipped.

Knowledge is hope
and endures with love.
Anti-Knowledge is fear
and holds onto hate.

Harley stared at the monster's back, frightened about what was about to happen next. There was one more page left to flip. He was tired and afraid he was losing his hope for freedom. With a deep sigh, he watched as the last page flipped over.

From the beginning and forever,
the most powerful energy
is love.

Harly looked up and watched the monster disappear over the wall as the ledge vanished. Immediately, he felt no longer bound to the chair. He jumped up and spun around, not seeing anything else in the round room.

Was I too terrified to move? Harley had fuzzy ideas that his bindings had been his doubts and fears. He scanned the round room and watched his chair become brittle, like dry papier mâché. It disappeared in micro bursts of thin white smoke as the cinder block wall surrounding him faded as if it was never there. The floor remained solid and gray, while a bluish, foggy haze surrounded the outside parameters and sky.

Harley spun toward the book. He watched the pages slowly dry up and become brittle enough so that the black ink seemed to weigh more than the white pages. Pieces of the book and finally the pedestal became flakes and dust as it all disintegrated, floating away like a ghost.

From where the pedestal and book used to be, the wall became thin and opaque enough for Harley to spy a thin person, about his height, standing on the other side. Was this what the monster was looking at? Was this the alien? He worried about where the monster went.

"You understand me, alien? Where am I?" Harley tried to keep his voice from shaking. He did not want to be afraid of the alien.

"I understand you. This place translates all languages. Before I tell you where you are, you must understand that I came from a solar system not seen by Earthian technologies." The alien's voice sounded dull and squeaky, like an irritating whistle.

"I don't care where you came from. I want to go back to where I was." Harley was fearing this fragile alien less as the wall disappeared completely.

He or she had a frail, pale complexion and thin arms and legs that were too long for the smooth, featureless body. The alien's hairless, oval head sat on shoulders in the absence of a neck and the small, round deep blue eyes were unfocused. He's no match for me in a fight, Harley decided.

"My spaceship brought you here. This is an intersection between Knowledge and your physical world."

"So what? I'm dead and this is purgatory? I'm to make amends for my wrong doings and go to heaven or hell? I'm not buying it 'cause I don't believe in heaven or hell. I believe there is one afterlife and a person can make it their personal heaven or hell if they want. But maybe there is an in between place between life and the afterlife. Except, I don't believe this is it."

"I'm not here to get involved in your species' religious beliefs. Humans use the concept of religion to promote God's love only as an instrument to promote hate and justify killing each other."

"Then why am I here talking to you?"

"You're here for me to study your death. I'll let you remember your death moment so you will stop arguing with me and we can continue with my study."

Harley's missing time slammed him with sharp, clear images of standing before a tall sunburned guy yelling at him. The guy had an oversized brass cross hanging around his neck as if it justified him being drunk and not liking Harley's more earthed colored face. They threw fists at each other for no other reason than it was a reason to let out their anger at being alone in a dirty, dark bar with cheap liquor.

They were too drunk to land fists hard against each other as the crowded bar erupted in cheers and quick bets were born. In a burst of frustrated anger, the sunburned guy pulled out an eight-inch dagger and thrust it deep into Harley's chest. The cheering went silent as Harley's blood gushed onto the dirty floor in rhythm to his heart. Harley sank like a deflated balloon as the alien light took him away.

"You are not dead—yet. I took your physical body before your soul left it. I wanted you to read my book as you died and give me more wisdom to add to it. Yet you are still alive. Something is in error."

"I don't care about your error, your study, the book, you, or your spaceship. If I was supposed to die, then you messed things up. Now that I'll live, I want outta here and you're not stopping me."

"I captured other species and studied their death. I recorded their final words in my book as they crossed their Threshold into an afterlife." The alien's face kept a blank expression, as if it was incapable of emotion.

"What has that got to do with me reading your book?"

"Human death is unique among the few species I have studied. Reading what I recorded was to motivate you to tell me more about love and the Knowledge as you died."

"Except I didn't die."

"Yes, the error I do not understand. Yet it is not my error, but yours. You are the failure."

"Wait a minute. I'm getting something here. From your book there is Knowledge and anti-Knowledge. Did your species follow the anti-Knowledge and you're scared there's no afterlife for you? I think you're studying death to find the path toward the Threshold." Harley felt a connection with the alien as if he could read the creature's mind.

"That is nonsense. I cannot be afraid of anything. I must not. My race has superiority in technology, government, and social norms. We must have an afterlife."

"Ha! I'll give you the superiority of technology, but politicians are all alike and social norms can be anything. Besides, don't you people come back from the dead? Like a near death experience? Or have people who can talk to the dead?" Harley got bored with the talking. He searched his surroundings, looking for an escape.

The alien stared at Harley as if debating what to do. "My species has no near-death experiences and we do not have individuals communicating with dead spirits. This does not prove we cease to exist at death. At least not for me. I am too important not to be immortal and exist in an afterlife. Why don't you die and show me how to cross over." The alien seemed to grin, except it looked like a painful grimace.

"What a bunch of garbage you're feeding me. I'm tired of listening to your nonsense."

The alien glowed green. Harley wondered if they would turn into the Incredible Hulk and confirm the ridiculous situation he found himself in. Behind the alien, Harley spied a jagged crack in the blue haze.

He ran his hand through his thin black curls on his head before continuing. "You stupid alien. There are so many people better at dying than me. I always planned to become a haunt, a wandering spirit, a ghost to torment the living on Earth. My personal purgatory. If you're trying to follow me to some type of threshold to the afterlife, it won't work."

Harley continued, seeing the alien in a new way. "Wow, I'm getting it now. You don't understand what the words in your book mean. You don't know what love is. Maybe you don't have an afterlife because you have no love. Maybe when you die, you sit in some purgatory place waiting for love that you refuse to accept until you vanish into nothing. A self-made, personal hell you think you deserve."

The alien turned a burning red. "I reject your premise. You were to transition into death and increase my knowledge of the afterlife so I could understand how to reach it. I do not want to talk about this nonsense of love."

"By the way, what about that monster? Was it your toy to keep me reading your book until I died?"

"That creature was a surprise to me and part of the error. Don't you know it is a fractured piece of yourself?"

"If that monster was part of me, then I'm glad it's out. Maybe it was why I was in a bar pushing down beer and whiskey in a place with men who cared too little for themselves. Their home had no love and no one to hold them when they got there. Like me."

Harley waited for a reaction from the alien, whose face had settled into a bored, bland expression. Like it had heard all this before.

He continued. "I believe in love. It's not something I ever had. Yet, it's my dream and hope. If I feared dying, it was because I was afraid there'd be no one to love me when I crossed over. Why would God have anything to do with my messed up self? Yet, you have shown me that maybe with love I will be all right on the other side of life."

The alien let out a meaningless sound that seemed to Harley as crying. The tormented person turned an orange color with their eyes becoming violet. The alien's vertical face puffed out like a balloon. "I do not need love. I have myself."

"I think you want love. Yet, that means rejecting the anti-Knowledge that your species accepted as the truth, even if it was an untruth," said Harley.

"You ugly human. You do not understand love any more than I," the alien said.

"I understand love because I never had any. I grew up with abuse, first by my dad with his fists until he left, then by my mom through her neglect. I turned out as they predicted because I didn't want to disappoint them." Harley felt better admitting this. The quick anger in him evaporated.

He continued. "I don't care about you. I didn't allow love in my life and that was my mistake."

He saw the bluish haze behind the alien become less dense and seem to beckon him to enter. Harley stomped past the alien and into the fading haze.

He entered a wide, pale yellow hallway, which led quickly to a short balcony without barriers. A grayness obscured the surrounding features. Down became a darker gray while up flowed as a grayer gray. He heard silence, smelled a lack of odors, and felt a slight warm wind like an icy heat.

"At least I'm still alive," he told himself, even though he could feel his heart beat slow and his breath become shallow.

A loud snort fell across his back and Harley spun around. The hideous monster stood a few feet away with its talons opened and spittle dropping from its crooked, green teeth. Its black eyes glared into Harley's. He accepted them as his own.

"I'm hungry," snarled the alter ego creature.

"Always hungry, like my old man. He was always hungry to use his fists on me until he left. I was always afraid my mother would find me another man like that to be my father. You are my fear and my childhood monsters who controlled me. Not anymore." Harley's voice disappeared up and down the hallway as he stared at the monster.

The frail alien walked down the hallway and stood next to the monster.

"You said I should find love, then I love this monster of yours. I love everything you do not want," the alien said.

"Go ahead and love that monster. He is my anger and hate. I don't want it anymore. Inside that creature are my fears I don't want them anymore, either." Harley felt confident and strong.

The monster had an ugly grin and pulled out an eight-inch dagger. Harley saw it as the same one he was stabbed with in the bar.

The alien laughed like a whimper and pointed at Harley, directing the monster to attack. The monster turned and pushed the blade deep into the alien's gut. The being sank like a deflated balloon.

Harley watched a soft pink glow shroud the alien and become a bright shimmering light as if multitudes of colorful jewels were taking the alien away. Then, the jewels darkened and became a dull black crowd of ant like creatures who faded away with the alien. Harley's monster lunged at him with the dagger.

He dodged the weapon and smashed his fist into the monster's neck. The dagger dropped as they clasped each other in anger and fear. They rolled over and over for an advantage until tumbling off the balcony and into the grasp of the grayness.

Struggling to get away from the monster, Harley kicked until the monster lost its grip. They flew apart from each other with the monster clawing the grayness for control of its flight downward.

Harley felt the denseness of his physical body keep him from flying into the brighter grayness. "It's time to die," he told his gray surroundings.

At that moment, Harley popped out of his physical self and watched his body fall back into the image of the dirty bar floor, which faded away, too. He floated into the brightening gray as the monster disappeared into the darker gray.

Harley did not know up or down, right or left. He felt infinite that he could exist between nothing and everything like this forever. For the first time in his life, Harley's fear and anger were gone as the torment of his life became a fading nightmare. He felt complete. Except, he began a painful trip wanting love.

Harley searched for someone else, some other soul he could talk to and not feel so alone in his peace and tranquility. He felt time flow in both directions around him and he accepted everything as bigger than him. He grew a feeling that something protected him and everything would be all right. Harley met a sphere of pallid colors pierced by daggers of dullness. Suddenly, the alien burst out of the sphere, grasping for Harvey.

"You were my hope to find love. I want to come with you."

"Stay away from me."

The alien lunged at Harley with open hands to hug or strangle him. Harley fled from the alien by falling higher into the grayness. He searched for the a crossover point or threshold and the loving hands of souls who would protect him and to take him away. He desperately wanted anyone to be there to love him. "I'm ready," he said, hoping someone was listening.

Harley lost the alien among the grayness, hoping they would find love. Maybe in a reincarnated life. He did not know how long he floated when his environment changed.

Within the gray, ribbons of pure rainbow colors slipped through. Harley believed his threshold was coming and he let himself float toward the bright multitude of colors.

The shock of the alien rushing at him from below made Harley scream. He ducked away from the alien's grasp, and continued toward the colors until falling into a gush of a raw wind. He screamed again as he smelled the sweat of a woman giving birth.

Nurses wrapped Harley's infant self in the most comfortable, warm, and softest blanket he ever will have. As he relished the comfort, he heard a baby crying. His mother had not finished giving birth and her screaming was short as another baby boy was born quickly. Harley's twin brother. The alien struggled to breathe.

Of course, he was human like himself and it took the nurses and a doctor several minutes before his brother was crying again. Harley knew at that moment his twin would need his care throughout their lives, and he was ready for it. They would learn about love together.

Finally cradled in their mother's arms, one on each side with Dad smiling down on them, Harley saw love in his parents' faces. He glanced at his twin brother, who smiled, too.

Bonus! Time Travel (for something unalien)

RETIREMENT 2039

Matthew opened his eyes and found himself floating in a light blue haze as if he had left his body and was looking for another. Around him bobbed yellow spheres the size of his fist that seemed to be as lost as he was.

He was not sure of anything, only that the time drug he took was supposed to let him relive a memory he selected. Matthew grew impatient with all the floating, thinking he had wasted his money. At that moment, one yellow sphere opened into a gaping dark hole. Matthew allowed himself to be swallowed inside.

He found himself in his nineteen-year-old body gripping the steering wheel of his new 1969 blue Ford Mustang convertible. It was the first car he owned and, with the top down, he could feel the Arizona heat flow over him.

He relaxed in the black bucket seats as he pushed on the accelerator. The power of the stroked engine sent him faster down the nearly empty Route 66 highway. Before him, the rippling heat distorted the asphalt into a long, thin line pointing him toward the distant Rockies.

On the other side of the mountains was his university where he would get his physics degree and eventually enter a career of sub-quantum theory. This time drug trip was a retirement gift to himself to help him forget that career.

Matthew remembered no outstanding, memorable accomplishments. Only a series of research papers and random accolades from his peers that kept him employed, but nothing that granted him fame.

In the future he came from, Matthew always had chill bumps and shivers across his wrinkled, thin dark skin and there was never enough light. Here in the desert, the dry heat warmed his youthful brown face and the brightness made him squint. He wanted to believe the feel of hot wind through the thick curls of his brown hair and that the sweat on his forehead was real.

He did not believe the time drug he swallowed seventy years in his future had really deposited him physically into this memory of his. It had to be a hallucination, although the experience felt real. At least I escaped for a little while from a future with more old people than young, he thought.

Matthew picked this memory because it was the best time in his life. It was when he escaped the boring Indiana corn fields, a drunken father, a cursing mother, and his cruel older brother Jacob. He felt free for the first time in his young life.

It was easy to be head of his high school class since half of them were more interested in smoking pot and having free sex. Also, having a low draft number for the Vietnam War convinced educators he was interested in a university education and not use the opportunity to avoid the draft. This encouraged local educators to help Matthew secured scholarships that covered most of his university expenses.

Local politicians were looking for a hero and someone to brag about who escaped the misery of a place offering a lot of nothing.

"If you get all that university education, you still won't be smart. All you'll have is a piece of fancy paperwork," Jacob told Matthew the morning of his high school graduation.

"I don't care what you think. I'm smarter than everyone in this county, including you. I'm never coming back here," Matthew yelled at his brother. Their parents stood next to Jacob in support.

"You're not getting far in a taxi," Matthew's father chuckled as his mother sneered.

Jacob had wrecked the family Chevy the evening before and it was Matthew's only ride to the university. As the three sat down to breakfast, Matthew got his packed bag and slipped out of the house unnoticed.

He had enough taxi money to get to the Ford dealership. They were always a Chevy family and Matthew felt good about buying the Mustang, even though the down payment took much of his savings.

He drove by the high school, picked up his diploma, and kept going. But not before driving past Cindy's house and blowing his horn until she came out.

"Yeah, see what you're missing? You'll be sorry you dumped me," he shouted at her.

"I didn't dump you. You kept ignoring me, so I ignored you, too. Are you going to keep ignoring me tonight at graduation?"

"I won't be there. I'm leaving this place for good. I'm headed for the university and a better future," said Matthew.

"Wait, I'm coming with you."

"No, you can't. I need to get out of this place now and I'm going alone. Enjoy graduation with all those losers."

Matthew drove until dusk and stayed in a motel over half the way to the university. The next morning after eating at a local diner, he made one phone call to Cindy and got no answer. He hoped she had fun at the graduation. He almost wished he had been there with her.

That morning on his way to the university was when he entered this memory of his youth. Matthew cradled the steering wheel with one hand as he stood up into the hot wind and shouted, "I'm free."

With the wind whipping across his face, he remembered the girls he would date at the university. His studies were always more important than relationships. He remembered it took him a long time to forget Cindy.

Matthew plopped back down as a few cars and pickups passed him going the other way. He passed a few cars going his way. Matthew wondered if they were AI images. If so, they were more real than he could imagine. He tried to figure out how everything could feel so real.

The drug company advertised that the time drug changed individual perceptions along arrows of time. The doctor who gave him the pill explained that the journey to his past was like going through higher dimensions of reversing causality and effect. Matthew didn't believe that. He took the drug to remember all the details of this time in his life.

After an hour, he arrived at a cluster of weathered buildings at the foothills of the Rockies. It was a crossover point with more grass and less desert. The one and two-story stone and adobe buildings could have been empty for all he knew.

Matthew pulled up to the same Esso gas station as when

he made this drive in his youth. Getting out, he spied a 'For Sale' sign hanging in the office window.

He remembered as a teenager how much he enjoyed working on cars. Matthew looked up at the mountains where a succession of university degrees would grant him titles in physics and he would never become a mechanic.

A dark, scarlet skinned man with graying temples approached the only pump. The label 'Owner' was stitched on his grease stained coveralls.

"How far is it to UCLA?" Matthew planned to take his time and enjoy his trip.

"Don't know. Never been there."

"Do you have a map or something?"

"Look inside for one."

Leaving the owner to pump gas and check his oil, Matthew walked into the front room dominated by a thick wooden desk holding a tall, heavy looking cash register. The place smelled of old oil, grease, and dry dirt. An opened doorway led to the one bay garage. At the back corner hung a restroom sign for anyone courageous enough to use the facilities.

Matthew picked up a map from a wall rack and unraveled it across the owner's greased stained desk. Before he could find the road toward UCLA, his eyes blurred.

He collapsed onto a squeaky swivel chair and closed his eyes to stop the vertigo. Images of himself, old and young, confused him. Matthew worried that the drug was wearing off. It was supposed to last until he reached the university.

He heard muffled voices and felt dull objects poke his chest. Matthew slit open his eyes and found himself on his back staring up into a surgical mask that stared back.

"How do you feel, Mr. Graves?" A woman's voice sounded squeaky.

"I want to go back," Matthew whispered.

"We lost you a couple of times, but I think you'll be all right now."

"What do you mean 'lost me'?"

"Your heart stopped, but we brought you around." A nearby man's voice sounded old.

"What year is it?"

After a pause, he said, "This is 2039. Your retirement year."

"No, it's 1969."

"Mr. Graves, your heart stopped for a few minutes, but we pulled you through," the woman repeated.

"I'm too young to be in 2039." Matthew could feel his nineteen-year-old youthfulness overcome a lingering fatigue.

He pulled himself up on his elbows enough to see his youthful reflection in a wall mirror. Matthew felt some urgency make him look to his right. He gasped at seeing his old self on the hospital bed next to him. This other self was barely breathing.

"What's going on here?" Matthew tried to sit up more, but he was too weak.

"Let's get him out of here," said the old voice. Strong hands tightened a bed sheet around Matthew and an orderly wheeled his bed out of the large room. They hurried him across the hall and into a smaller room with a single red recliner against a wall.

After the orderly left, Matthew struggled to get out of his bedsheet. He could feel his strength emerging in layers. He wanted to go back to the other room and find out what was going on. He felt some connection with his older self and was confused at how he could be nineteen again.

Matthew loosened the bed sheet and was about to get up

when the door swung open. The tall doctor with unwrinkled skin and a ponytail who gave him the pills strode in. "Matthew, I'm here to explain what is happening to you."

Behind this man shuffled in another man bent with age with multiple wrinkles dug into his pale skin. He settled cautiously into the recliner. A third, slightly wrinkled orderly stood beside the door.

"Explain it then." Matthew's confusion transgressed quickly toward anger.

"We can provide a longer explanation later. For now, the drug linked your present self with the memory of your past self."

"Then this made two of me? How is this possible? My past was only a memory." Matthew wondered how much of what the man said was true.

The old man in the recliner spoke in a gravelly voice. "It is our theory that a person living through an important part of their life, bad or good, creates permanent impressions in time and space. For you, that memory you went back to was when you felt free from family and rural life. Part of who you are today went back to that memory seventy years ago."

"This doesn't make sense," Matthew said.

"Just understand that we're excited about our success with you," said the ponytail doctor. "You are our first patient to have your past consciousness return with the body of your youth and be alive."

"We did this by keeping your older self alive," said the older man. "By doing so, you remained tethered to the present. When the time drug wore off, your past consciousness snapped back to now and brought your physical body along. You materialized out of an oval blue hole beside your old body. Except, your heart was not beating in your younger self, just like the others."

Matthew wondered if he had died and none of this was real.

"We resuscitated your young body and soon your old body will die making you young again in the now," the doctor said.

"How can I be two people at the same time?"

The older man said, "This is where we leave science and talk about souls. We think your soul is straddling both bodies, linking them together. However, our analysis shows the link weakening. What remains of your present soul is migrating into your younger body, which is stronger. You should be back at work in a few weeks."

"No. I might end up with this young body, but I'm retired."

"No, we will cancel your retirement since you are young again," said the ponytail.

Matthew's fists clench the loose white sheets covering him. "You can't do that. I've already worked my whole life. If this is real, then I want to use this youth for myself."

"That's selfish, don't you think?" The older man said with a smirk.

"It's not selfish to work a lifetime and want to enjoy retirement." Matthew pushed himself up on his elbows, but the younger doctor easily pushed him back down. The orderly took a step closer. Matthew's strength was coming back, slowly. He pretended he was still weak.

"As you know, in our age there are more old people than young and the population is down overall. There's no one to carry on the work and sustain what we built. Since you had no children, it's fair to put you back to work." The doctor's tone grew determined.

"You can leave now, doctor. I'll finish explaining," said the old man in the recliner.

The ponytail quickly left the room, leaving the orderly standing by the door. Matthew could feel more of his strength returning, yet he kept still waiting for the moment to act. He worried that as he got stronger, his older self was becoming weaker in the other room.

"Population continues to decline. We need a new workforce and the only way to do that is to harvest the past. The time drug will be our fountain of youth. You're the result of years of research to break the paradoxes of time switching," said the old man.

"Who are you? You can't change the laws of physics. Cause and effect must remain. I don't see how any of this can happen," said Matthew.

"That memorable event in your life will continue to exist even if you aren't there to experience it. Just like a video on repeat."

"Go on and explain more." Matthew thought some of this sounded familiar.

"Granted, we've still got a lot to learn. But I want to be the first to thank you for helping this experiment succeed."

"I had nothing to do with this." Matthew wanted to escape, but where would he go?

"In your academic life, you theorized a fifth energy source existing in the sub-quantum world. Using blue lasers and absolute cold led us to discover a string of motionless bubbles separated by positions in time and space," said the elderly man.

"You used my research without me knowing?" Matthew thought the old man looked like someone he should know, but he could not place him.

"Yes, and it was instrumental in building our theories and

furthering our research. We discovered that, throughout a person's life, there are impressionable life moments creating bubbles within time and space. The moments are like short films existing in the sub-quantum world." The old man took a few deep breaths, as if the explanation exhausted him.

"I remembered those theories, but I never believed them," said Matthew.

"Maybe the bubbles are frozen parallel universes. We don't know. All we know is that the drug alters mental senses and sends at least part of a soul into the past to capture and pull the physical to the present."

The old man nested further into his red recliner. Looking older, he continued, "I think the time drug works because the soul is your fifth energy source. The drug alters the mind's currents, agitates subspace matrices, and changes the super spin of pseudo energy particles. In simpler terms, the time drug helped your soul split between both of your physical bodies. One in the present with the one in the past. No worries. As you grow stronger, your older body will die and your soul will be one again in that young body."

"What this means is that I work until I get old, then you trade me for another of my younger memories until I run out of former lives to remember." Matthew felt strong enough to get off his bed, yet he stayed still.

"That's correct. But you should be happy. You get to live many lives," said the aged man.

"Who are you?"

"I always thought you were smarter than me, but all you've done is let people use you and your work." The old man trembled as a soft laughter enveloped him.

"You're Jacob?" Matthew could not believe this was his older brother.

"I spent my youth taking care of our aging parents and I used them for my income. They did not need much to live on and, when they finally died, they left me wealthy. Except I lost my youth. So, I invested in your research. You doubted yourself too much, but I knew you could discover time travel," Jacob said.

"Are you going to relive your past?"

"I'll take the time drug and come back like you because I don't think just going into the past and staying there will work. The soul of the past needs to return and unite with the soul of the present. Once I come back and before my older self dies, I'll give my older self a second pill so he will die and break the tether. At the same time, I'll take second pill and return permanently to my past. When I'm there, I'll remember the future and make sure to enjoy life much better and wealthier."

Jacob took out a small box and fondled it in his wrinkled hand. "For you, all we have to do is wait for your older self to die naturally. Then, you'll be ready to return to work for another seventy years."

Matthew threw off the bedsheet and swung his feet off the bed. He slugged the charging orderly in the nose, sending him backward in a face of blood. Matthew lunged at his brother and easily snatched the pillbox from his brother's weak grip. He ran out of the room.

Matthew found his unattended, older body lying on a hospital bed looking back at him. The unsettling situation made him uncertain whether he was standing, lying down, or what his true thoughts were. In his youthful body, he was willing to take risks, yet his older self hesitated about what to do. Matthew wanted to run and live, but also to stay and die.

Quickly, the young Matthew shoved one pill into his older self while swallowing the second pill. His older self understood and swallowed. The younger Matthew felt weightlessness as his older self gasped a final breath. Matthew became aware of the death moment and the effect ran to his sense of being.

The young Matthew's surroundings disappeared in a swirl of deepening blue. Tinges of yellow spikes brought undistinguishable patterns which evoked confusing emotions. There were many things to see, but his three-dimensional mind could not fully experience them.

Slowly, Matthew's eyes focused on a map in his young hands. Dry heat bathed his face and alarms sounded distantly in his ears until they became a slight ringing that went away. He sat there enjoying the simple, dry desert air. Looking up, instead of the station owner Cindy stomped in.

"I'm glad I finally caught up to you before you got to that university. I would have lost you in that place. If you want to go on and get that learning, I'm good with that as long as you promise to stop ignoring me."

"What are you doing here?" Matthew stood to face Cindy.

"I'm here to love you. We're supposed to be together. Don't you know that?"

"Yeah, I know that now."

Matthew breathed in Cindy's soft kiss. When they parted, they held each other close and Matthew asked, "Would you like to live here?"

"I always loved the desert and the mountains. Indiana has cold and snow. What's your plan?"

The station owner walked in. "I think I gave you two long enough to say hello. Your cars are gassed up and ready."

"How about I give you that Mustang and some cash for this gas station?"

"I don't want to take advantage of you, but what the hell.

It's a deal."

The owner took off his grease stained coveralls and tossed them to Matthew who tossed the former gas station owner the car keys. Cindy gave Matthew a long hug.

In the next few weeks, they cleaned up the gas station with plans to sell sandwiches and soda pop. They also planned their wedding.

Matthew knew he would be a good mechanic in this desert town near the mountains. And without his research, no one would be coming back for him.

The Disease

Susan sat by her son's hospital bed for half an hour before an orderly swung back the heavy curtain partition. "I'm sorry. We need the room for another patient."

She searched the young man's face and saw tiredness from all the deaths. "What are you doing with his body?"

"You know it has to be cremated, the same as all the bodies who died from the disease."

There was only one viral disease people talked about. Otherwise, they said "not the disease" and few people said that. She let go of her seventeen-year-old son's cold hand after seven hours of watching him die. She wanted a proper burial for Nathan and not be given a heavy plastic bag of his ashes when they got around to burning his body.

"I'm immune, so why wasn't he?" She wanted answers. They were not coming from this impatient orderly who was obviously immune, too.

"Ma'am, please. A lot of people have gathered in the cafeteria to talk about their losses. Why don't you join them?"

Susan hated his politeness. Nathan was that polite and respectful, so why did he die? She left her son's body to be erased from existence and walked outside to a blue sky and warm air. On such a beautiful day in late May, they would have gone on one of their long walks in the nature park near their suburban home. Instead, she watched another ambulance drive in, no longer bothering with sirens.

This one was a retrofitted delivery van from a popular retailer. Real ambulances were used for other patients. She wondered if the company charged for shipping.

Driving home in her pickup truck, the online radio came on automatically. It was tuned to a female voice announcing the number of survivals from the disease. Once someone got the disease, they recovered in an hour or so or were dead in forty-eight hours. Like Nathan, her husband Sam died the first of May simply by drifting off to sleep. Some people wished they got the disease and died that easily. Susan also wished they got the disease instead of her son and husband. She flipped the radio off.

Susan drove through two suburbs to get home. It was a fifty minute drive that gave her too much time alone. When she got home, her time alone became infinite.

The cable news said how only one tenth of a percent of the population died from the disease. There were more deaths from other diseases and many people recovered. It was enough to keep down panic and almost everyone went back to their normal lives.

To Susan, knowing these facts just made her angry. She could not see herself returning to a normal life, ever. She opened a bottle of merlot and took a few gulps from the bottle before sitting on the edge of Nathan's bed.

"I hate you, Sam. Nathan was so much like you and I

thought he wouldn't be like you and die from the disease. I thought he would have been like me and survive," she told the quiet bedroom. Her voice echoed against the plaster walls and ceiling, and the wood floor. She took more gulps of wine.

An hour later, she got up with an empty bottle and threw it at the mirror showing the dark bags under her brown eyes. If she untied her long black hair from the ponytail, the texture would cause it to fling out in all directions. Susan left it tied and staggered into the extra bedroom she used as her writing room. She scanned the bookshelf with her published dystopian books.

Her author income was enough to supplement Sam's and give them the finances to afford the house that now was hers alone. Susan ran from the room and through the house looking for matches to set fire to her books.

When did matches become obsolete? She stood in the kitchen and screamed. No one would hear her through the soundproof walls, which was when she remembered her research for a time travel book she wrote last year.

The scientist was eccentric and alone with his research after being shunned by his peers. To Susan, he sounded convincing as if he had really invented a time travel machine. He let her use the recorded conversation between them in her book. She thought it was the reason her dystopian book was her bestseller.

The wine caught up to Susan and she slept on the couch for hours until the house grew dark. When she woke up, she knew exactly what she had to do. It was her only hope.

She grabbed a large trash bag and ransacked her bedroom and bathroom for what she would need for the next few days. Before leaving, she turned off the water to the house and threw the main circuit breaker off in case she did not come back.

At the gas station where she filled up, Susan bought a handful of power bars, energy drinks, and a large coffee. It would be a long night and she planned to stop only for gas.

From Dayton, Ohio, the city of inventions, to Baltimore, Maryland, the city where the scientist Praveen lived, took almost eight hours. Driving up to his inner city house, she thought he should be more careful about his online identity and personal life.

It was a small rambler needing a new roof and the shrubs looked like large weeds. The rising sun pushed against an overcast gray sky. Susan always liked sunrises and thought this was a good omen as she cut off the engine.

It took five series of three poundings before Praveen jerked open the door. "Who are you? What do you want?"

"I'm Susan. You helped me with my time travel research on one of my dystopian novels. I want to travel back in time to save my son from dying of the disease." She thought it was too late for Sam.

"Right to the point. Just like when we talked about my research. I'm living here alone after my wife died from the disease two weeks ago. You can come in or run away."

Susan followed Praveen and found herself in his kitchen. "This is a weird house. The entryway is into the kitchen."

"My wife and I enjoyed cooking. Why not?"

She sat at the kitchen table, which took the place of a kitchen island, and enjoyed the smells of past spicy food baked into the warm air. It made her sad for Praveen's wife. She took a deep breath. "I'm sorry for your loss."

"I'm sorry for the loss of your son."

"And my husband three weeks ago. I can't get over their

deaths. Like everyone, I believed what I was told and the death rates were too low to be cautious. I should have paid more attention and now my son and husband are dead. I managed with Sam's death as long as I had Nathan. When he died and Sam being gone for so long, I believe I have a chance to at least get my son back. That's why I'm here."

"It was no use paying attention to the data about the disease. It wouldn't have stopped your family's deaths, just like it didn't stop my wife's death. And now you want to travel back in time to do what?"

"I don't know. I'll figure it out when I get there. Maybe I can warn the medical experts about what's coming. I have to do something." Susan was getting hungry from the rich aromas in the kitchen. It was as if Praveen's wife was there cooking breakfast.

"How do you know I have a time machine?"

"You sent me the design and diagrams to put in my novel, which I should have. They looked pretty real."

Praveen sat at the table across from Susan. "You want something to drink? I have a bottle of cabernet. It's a screw top."

"Yeah, sounds good. I'm still buzzing from all the caffeine."

"All I have are red plastic cups." Praveen poured their liquid breakfast.

They swallowed two gulps of wine before Praveen said, "The design was based on creating a quantum loop around a glass cylinder. Inside the cylinder I rotated in the opposite direction a silver cylinder where someone should be able to travel backward in time, up to a limit."

"That sounds as if it would take a lot of power."

"Other scientists believed that, too. That's the secret. My

lasers need very little energy to nudge a few atoms into a quantum state." Praveen proudly smiled at Susan.

Susan took two more swallows from her cup, emptying it. "Do you have this time machine nearby?"

Praveen finished his cup and pointed toward the basement door. He poured Susan and himself the rest of the wine before continuing.

"I can turn it on and my instruments show what it's supposed to do. But I don't know what happens on the inside and if any contents would travel in time or not."

"Why weren't you tempted to get into the machine and prevent your wife's death?"

"The controls are outside of the machine. I would need to teach someone how to work them. Also, there is a lot of uncertainty and I could be wrong about everything." Praveen stared at his red cup. "I was afraid."

Susan felt bad for Praveen. Yet, she was focused. "Can you control how far back to send someone?"

"A person can go back only as far as their own timeline. I can control how far that is by adjusting the laser energy. When a person travels back in time, I theorized the vibrations in their body matches the timeline they're going to. Meanwhile, a quantum link keeps the person tied to the now so they can come back."

"I want to get into your silver cylinder." Susan gulped down her wine while staring at Praveen.

"I knew you'd say that. I don't want to be accused of murder if you die. Also, what if it works? There are all the paradoxes. Aren't you afraid?"

"Yeah, sure. I know this is grief driving me to do this and risk my life, but I need to get into your time machine and at least try." Susan had her doubts, yet she saw no other way to save her son and she did not want to live any longer without him. Like Sam, she felt the longer Nathan was dead the harder it would be to change history.

Praveen gulped down the rest of his wine. "This is what I think. When you go back, two of you cannot exist in the same time period. I think your younger self will become frozen an instant before your arrival and stay there until you vacate the time period."

"How will I come back?"

"You must be at the exact place where you found yourself. Assuming you are still alive to bring you back, I will gradually decrease the power in the lasers and cool down the quantum link. You would be pulled back to the present and your younger self will continue along her timeline in a normal way as if nothing happened."

"I know there are more risks than either of us can think about. I need to do something even if it changes me. Even if I die." Susan drummed her fingers on the table that she did when anxious.

"I haven't agreed to do this," Praveen said. His face fell and he grew quiet. After a few moments, he continued. "You and I are grieving. You want to take risks and I want to be safe."

"Think of it this way. This could be your only chance to see if your time machine works or not."

Praveen stared at his empty cup. "Sometimes, I wished I had not invented it."

Neither spoke for almost a minute until Praveen said, "Okay, let's do this. I'll send you back as far as I can safely do. I think it will be before the disease begins to spread. I'll give you three hours before I begin cooling down the quantum link to bring you back."

"If I succeed and get scientists to stop the disease, will I come back into the universe I left or a parallel universe?"

"I don't know. I don't know a lot about everything. There are too many possibilities."

"I want to try, anyway."

"I want you to try since it may save my wife. She was pregnant with our first child."

Susan got up and opened the basement door. She waited for Praveen to follow her, which took him only a few seconds to decide.

In the basement, a few narrow windows at the ceiling level brought in some daylight to meet the neon lighting. The basement was empty except for a six foot high glass cylinder with a silver cylinder inside. It sat on a ceramic concave nest in the center of the basement. Three metal tubes resting on squat stands surrounded the cylinders with each pointed toward the middle of the glass cylinder. Thin electrical cords from the back of the tubes entwined themselves across the concrete floor to a generator with the exhaust attached to the wall and likely outside.

Susan hoped she could fit inside the silver cylinder. Not eating much as her husband, then her son die, helped. Miniature tubes laced the glass cylinder meandering within the glass. A pale syrupy goo crawled inside the tubes.

"They're my mix of bacteria," said Praveen, walking over to a fold out table. He powered up three laptops.

"Why bacteria?"

"They're my secret sauce. They are my modified non-sulfur bacteria found at local saltwater beaches. My theory is that their energetic compounds exist at the quantum level and help create a proper vibrating link."

"What about the lasers?"

"The three low energy lasers cause a loop of energy

surrounding the glass. They interact with the bacteria and create an inverse of energy within the glass cylinder. It sits on a gallium arsenide concave base coated in a high carbon, pressurized ceramic mixture. The interaction of excited photons causes the glass cylinder to free float in a superconductivity state."

"Then what happens?"

"The loops drag photons around the cylinder, making it spin until stretching the fabric of the space-time continuum. Inside the glass cylinder, the silver cylinder spins in the opposite direction using electromagnetic forces underneath and above."

Susan approached the glass cylinder and her breath caused the cylinder to rotate slightly. Praveen came over after turning on the laptops. She heard a whirring noise from the tubes.

"Everything is activated and working within the norms. You want to hear more about the science?"

"No. Truthfully, I didn't understand some of what you explained already. And it doesn't really matter. Can you help me get inside?"

Praveen looked at Susan. "I don't want to hurt you. I certainly don't want to murder you."

"I'm not blaming you for anything that happens to me. I need to go back and save my son. And my husband if that's possible. And your wife and unborn child. You've got to help me."

Praveen got a stool and helped Susan squeeze through a narrow slit in the glass and into a small door within the silver cylinder. Neither spoke. Susan sat in a crouch position, shifting her body around to be as comfortable as possible. Praveen stood at the open hatchway, wringing his hands in worry.

"Don't you die on me."

"I promise you this will be a success." Susan gave Praveen a slight smile. She tried not worry about what death would be like in a time machine.

Susan watched Praveen's face cycle through multiple expressions. He looked like he was debating, arguing, and disagreeing with himself about what could or could not happen.

"Close it up, Praveen. Next stop my past."

He clicked the hatch on the silver cylinder closed, enveloping her in total darkness. In less than a minute, Susan felt the cylinder slightly vibrate.

Susan found herself naked on the kitchen floor of the Baltimore condo where she, Sam, and Nathan lived before moving to Ohio. Sitting up, she took three deep breaths to calm herself down. She never believed the time travel thing would happen, or leave her nude.

Looking at packed boxes and a mostly empty condo, Susan knew that Sam and Nathan had already moved to Dayton several weeks ago in late August so Nathan could start school on time. Sam had already started his transfer job and she had another week before following them to Ohio. The media would report the first cases of the disease in China in a week and nine months later Sam and Nathan would die from it.

She was not far from Praveen's house, yet she had no plans to see him. Instead, she dug out some clothes from a box and took an almost empty city bus to the university famous for molecular biology and public health. In this past, she had just finished a class to keep her certification as a psychoanalyst. She was successful as an author, yet not confident enough to rely only on her creativity.

Doctor Schmidt was a well known department head in the Molecular Biology department with influence among

Washington D.C. politicians. Most particularly with the staff working for the National Institute of Allergy and Infectious Diseases. Forty minutes later, Susan knocked on his office door.

"Student hours are over. Come back this afternoon."

Susan swung the door open, revealing a room big enough for a small desk, three narrow shelves of neatly arranged books, and two vinyl chairs for guests. Dr. Schmidt looked up from his monitor sitting in the corner of his wooden desk.

His black curly hair came off his scalp as if not knowing which direction to go. Some of it browsed his ears. His brown eyes glared at Susan with suspicion.

"Do I need to call security? Are you a student here? You're not in any of my classes."

"I want to talk to you about a coming epidemic."

"Ever since COVID, people have been obsessed with epidemics. Why don't you write a dystopian novel about your premonition and get out of my office?"

Susan sat in one of the guest chairs. "In a week, the first cases of a deadly virus will be detected in China. It will not be classified as an epidemic."

"And you know this how?"

"There's a scientist named Praveen who built a time machine. He sent me back in time so I might stop the virus. I took a class here and remembered your background and credentials." Susan knew this was a long, long shot and she hoped Schmidt did not call security.

The doctor leaned back in his chair and folded his hands behind his head. He eyed Susan with pinched eyebrows. "So, you thought my political connections can get people to believe in an epidemic like COVID coming from a time traveler? Don't say anything." He held his hands toward Susan. "I know Praveen and his work. Is this a joke for him to get more funding?"

Susan eyed Schmidt, wondering if he accepted the concept of time travel. "No joke. Nine months from now, my son will die from the disease. My husband before him. Also, Praveen's pregnant wife. I know this is crazy and if I were you I wouldn't believe any of what I'm saying. Except I'm not leaving until you do." Even if it meant missing going back to my present, she thought. Praveen never said what would happen if she missed her return.

"His time machine is not that improbable. Some scientists here have secretly been helping him develop it further. But transferring a physical body—I don't think that is possible."

"But, I'm here."

"I think your future soul is here while your body remains in the future. You simply co-exist somehow with the physical body of your past. This is why no one talks about Praveen's experiments. We scientists would have to admit souls exist. Frankly, I'm nervous about him playing around with souls like that. I do believe in God."

"I don't know what to say. That would explain how I so easily went from my future to my past." It made sense to Susan since she had a hard time believing her physical self could travel through time.

"Before we discuss Praveen's time machine anymore, tell me about the virus."

Susan explained everything she knew about the disease. She talked about the facts and theories, the deniers until they lost family members, and the politicians downplaying the seriousness of the disease so they could be re-elected. Most importantly, the lack of a vaccine because the deaths were not high enough to hit the epidemic threshold. Although many thought there were more deaths than reported. Still, the pharmaceutical companies would not have a high enough profit and the conservative government did not believe in science.

As she talked, Schmidt typed notes into his computer. When Susan finished, she asked, "What can you do?"

"How is the virus transmitted?"

"Medical researchers believe it's spread the same as any flu. Tiny droplets emitted by infected people when they cough, sneeze, or talk after they become sick."

"Some facts interest me. Few people get sick and the ones who do there's a high percentage of deaths. I think the virus could be attacking certain groups of people based on their inherited traits. That would cause a high death level for some cultures and not others, causing an overall low average. Those of western and northern Europe, along with the Slavic classes seem to be less affected than people descended from the Middle East, Africa, and South America. I'm not certain about Asia."

"My son and husband died, also Praveen's wife. That's enough deaths for me to be concerned." Susan let the anger in her voice show.

"I apologize. I'm trying to understand this disease because it's not like other viruses that infect humans."

"So, you believe me. Can you stop it from spreading? That's all I care about."

"I can't promise you anything, but I know the people who can help. I need to go where the virus started and I already have plans to fly to China tomorrow to meet with other researchers on our annual collaboration. I'm not saying I totally believe you, but my Chinese friends owe me a favor and it would not hurt to check things out. Research acknowledged that COVID came from a Chinese farmer catching it from the animals he lived with. Maybe the same could be true with this virus."

"Praveen will restart the time machine soon. I need to be in the same place to be picked up. I don't want to leave without knowing you can save my son and husband and Praveen's pregnant wife."

"Go back. I don't know what will happen if you stay in this timeline. No offense, but I don't want my future changed because you're here."

On the bus, she was uneasy at how quickly she succeeded in getting help. It was almost as if destiny was real and had pushed her in this direction to find Doctor Schmidt. Susan did not know what else to do. Except, if Schmidt didn't stop the disease when she went back, she'd try again. Even if it meant ending up in a different timeline. All she wanted was to be in a timeline where Nathan and Sam were alive. She sighed at the empty seat beside her on the bus.

At the condo, Susan took off her clothes and put them back into the moving box. She looked around and saw everything was in its place. She remembered the excitement they all felt with this move. Nathan had not been happy in his high school with no friends. The move gave him hope for a new beginning.

Susan sat on the floor thinking about her son having a future if Schmidt was successful. She thought of Sam. Sitting there, she felt a slight vibration tremble through her naked body. Susan felt herself spinning in place and she wanted to vomit.

It may have been hours, minutes, or seconds before she opened her eyes to stare at the darkened inside of the cylinder. She was naked as Praveen opened the hatch.

"I can't believe this worked," he said, finding a blanket for

Susan as he helped her out of the cylinder. She plopped into a nearby chair.

"How do you feel?" Praveen gave her a brush for her unruly hair.

"I feel dizzy and a little sick to my stomach, but okay." The tangles were hard to get out. She gave up and handed the brush back to Praveen.

"No headache or tingling anywhere? Here's some cold water."

"No, nothing like that. Has anything changed? I met with a Doctor Schmidt."

Praveen had a look of shock. He took three steps back with widening eyes and his mouth hung down.

"What's wrong? Do you know Schmidt?"

"Are you sure you met with him?"

"Yes, I'm positive." Susan described the doctor.

"Researchers believe he was patient zero or the index case for the disease. He was the first one to die while in China. Many researchers believed he wasn't the source of the virus and that someone gave it to him in Baltimore before he traveled to China. He was already sick when he arrived. Our government and the media refuted that since no one got sick in Baltimore and China was wrongly blamed."

Susan jumped up. "Doctor Schmidt believed in your time machine, but he said I didn't physically travel in time."

"He was wrong. My sensors showed you faded away. You went into your past."

"No, I didn't physically go into my past."

"Why did you think you had no clothes on when you arrived in your past? They were destroyed in the passage. Didn't you look in a mirror and see you were from this time period?" Praveen's face contorted into an expression of horror.

"It can't be true that I infected Doctor Schmidt." Susan's face joined Praveen's with the realization about what she had done. Susan dropped back in the chair, hugging her blanket. "This makes me responsible for the death of my son and my husband and everyone else, including your wife and unborn child."

Praveen brought over a chair and sat across from Susan. "It's not your fault, but mine. I should never have invented the time machine and sent you back." He hung his face in his hands and cried.

Susan looked up. "Wait a minute. Maybe our destiny can be changed. We still have the time machine. What if I go back and leave myself a note explaining everything and not visit Schmidt?"

Praveen said nothing for a few seconds, before responding. "You can't go back and neither can I. You're a carrier and I would be, too. If it isn't Doctor Schmidt, it would be someone else. You could think you're being careful, but you won't."

"Then, what? I should have never tried to change the past." Susan pounded her fists against her thighs and cried in frustration. Praveen brought his face out of his hands.

"What if I go back and stop myself from building the time machine? This has all been about the disease, but not about the machine. I can go back and destroy some of the paperwork, so it will be difficult for my past self to continue. I was working on another project and I was never excited about this one. This could break the loop, meaning my present self never existed to build something that would infect anyone in the past."

"Will you be killing yourself?"

Praveen stood up sharply. "I think I would merge with

myself in another timeline. I need to show you how to operate the equipment."

Twenty minutes later, Susan understood enough to send Praveen back in time. Standing in front of the cylinder, they made final plans.

"Give me two hours before you turn the lasers off. That will close the time loop."

"Is that enough time?" Susan worried about how any of this would work.

"I don't know if two hours is enough. But I don't want to stay in the past too long and risk infecting someone else if I'm not successful in stopping myself from building the time machine."

They had nothing else to say to each other. After Praveen crammed himself inside, Susan did not hesitate to close the silver door and run the sequences to fire up the lasers. The glass enclosure with the strange bacteria spun around as the silver cylinder went in the opposite direction.

Susan stood in the basement for several minutes. Outside, she heard traffic move down the urban street and an air conditioner turn on to blow cool air into her face from a ceiling vent. It was a warm day for the end of May.

She paced the basement, read some of Praveen's papers scattered about that she did not understand, then sat down to wait. When it was time, she powered down the lasers. With everything still, she carefully opened the silver cylinder door. Praveen was not there.

Someone upstairs clanged pots around, and the smell of the spicy aromas flowed from the kitchen. Before she got to the banister, Praveen came down the basement stairs.

"You need to go home," he said.

Susan wordlessly pointed at the time machine that was not there. Her cell phone rang.

"Mom, my locator says you're in Baltimore. What are you doing there?"

"Nathan?"

"Yeah, who else? When and why did you go to Baltimore?"

Susan took a deep breath to calm herself. "I'll explain everything to you and your dad later. I'll call back in a little bit." She wondered how much they would believe. She was having a hard time believing any of it.

Susan looked at Praveen. "Do you remember me?"

"No, but my future self left plenty of notes for me to find. At this moment, our time loops are closed and we exist as one. The loop with the time machine collapsed and is no more. You are the only one to remember everything."

"Is it possible I was never patient zero and there was no disease?" Susan leaned on the banister and cried with relief.

"Years ago, I had two decisions to make. One was the time machine and another was development of a new energy to replace fossil fuels. The notes left for me helped me choose the latter. I never developed the time machine and I never will. Now, you need to go home. My wife doesn't understand. She's out back in our herb garden."

Susan got into her pickup, yet the dashboard was different. Praveen knocked on her side window that she rolled down.

"Here is a list of instructions on how to manipulate the fuel. The government is giving these out on all vehicles retrofitted with the new fuel I invented."

"If you invented a new fuel, why aren't you rich like Rockefeller?"

"My name in Hindu means 'expert' and 'skilled' which does not mean I want to be rich. I made sure I worked with the university, so the patent is shared by everyone."

Susan smiled. "I think I want to stop writing dystopian novels. I want to write a story like this with a happy ending."

Praveen smiled. "Have a great trip home to your husband and your son."

About the Author

Thank you for reading my science fiction short stories.

After a childhood on a Virginia dairy farm, I spent over three decades working in the Pentagon which qualified me to write science fiction. I have had almost thirty of my stories published in magazines and journals and I self-published several novels, all different. This guarantees me no author success as a brand name. Like Studs Terkel wrote, "Hope dies last."

I live in eastern North Carolina where I belong to writing groups, teach a creative writing class at the library, and volunteer at nonprofits to include writing grants.

More about me can be found at https://stanleybtrice.com/. Please visit and sign up for my newsletter! I try to be different.

I hope you enjoyed *Eight Stories Aliens Will Believe*. Please try out my other books. I like all of them. More are coming.

Peace begins with a smile. — *Mother Theresa*